JUN - - 2021

10

TRUTHS

AND A

DARE

10 TRUTHS AND A DARE

ASHLEY ELSTON

HYPERION

Los Angeles   New York

First Edition, May 2021
10 9 8 7 6 5 4 3 2 1
FAC-020093-21078
Printed in the United States of America

This book is set in Fairfield LT Std/Monotype
Designed by Shelby Kahr

Library of Congress Control Number: 2021930713
ISBN 978-1-368-06238-1

Reinforced binding

Visit www.hyperionteens.com

For the Classes of 2020 and 2021

10
TRUTHS
AND A
DARE

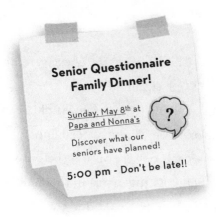

Senior Questionnaire
Family Dinner!

Sunday, May 8th at
Papa and Nonna's

Discover what our
seniors have planned!

5:00 pm - Don't be late!!

Truth #1: If something happens but your nonna doesn't find out about it and tell the whole family, then it didn't really happen

Sunday, May 8th, Afternoon

Olivia

Almost every milestone in my life is in some way attached to my grandparents' house. First steps? Four right down the main hallway. First lost tooth? Stuck in a caramel apple Nonna had waiting for us in the kitchen after trick-or-treating. First kiss? Jason McAfee, who was friends with my cousin Charlie and Wes from next door, in the attic playing spin the bottle in eighth grade.

So when it was time to fill out the senior questionnaire, there was no question where we would gather.

"Okay, does everyone have a pencil?" Nonna asks from her spot at the head of the table.

Next to me, Charlie pats his chest several times, then scans the floor. "I've lost mine."

Nonna rolls several to me. "Olivia, please pass these to Charlie and anyone else who may need one."

Charlie tests each one I give him before settling on the one he wants, then puts the extras in the middle of the table.

"Is it weird I'm doing this?" our cousin Sophie asks. "I mean, I'm glad I'm here, but it's not like I have anyone to turn this in to."

"You'll turn it in to me and I'll keep it with the others," Nonna answers, pointing toward the fabric-covered box sitting on the edge of the kitchen counter. Then she winks at Wes, who is sitting next to Sophie, across the table from me. "I want a copy of yours, too."

Wes beams and scratches his full name at the top of his sheet, then sits poised and ready for Nonna to start.

Uncle Sal is leaning against the counter on the far side of the kitchen, a piece of paper, rumpled and stained, dangling from his fingers. "If the twins aren't here in the next five minutes, we're starting without them."

Nonna glances at the clock, then at the back door, before looking at Sal. "Maggie Mae said they would be here."

Uncle Sal rolls his eyes and goes back to his phone.

In this family, my grandmother has the final word. And filling out the questionnaire is no different.

Our high school seems to pride itself on traditions as much as she does. When this first started fifty-eight years ago, there were only a few basic questions for seniors: *Will you go to college? If so, where? What is your dream job?* But the questionnaire has taken on a life of its own. Now the school wants to know your favorite memory and your most embarrassing one, your favorite charity and one thing about the world you wish you could change, and on and on and on. The answers are shared across the big white screen that hangs from the ceiling while we march one by one in cap and gown. Nonna has kept a copy of every sheet every member of our family has ever completed. And since all of us, except Sophie and her older sister, Margot, graduated from the same high school, she has a sheet on everyone.

And now it's A Thing. A thing that once a year becomes part of Sunday family supper. A thing where the current seniors fill it out in front of everyone and then we compare it to our parents' answers. And our aunts' and uncles' answers. And our cousins' answers.

You get the point.

Sophie might not have to do it for her school, but she has to do it for Nonna, just like Margot did. And since Wes is an honorary member of this family, there was no way he was getting out of it either.

Not that they feel especially put out. In fact, they seem

downright tickled to be here. Or maybe it's because they're always tickled to be with each other, no matter what the activity is or where we are.

While Nonna looks at Sophie and Wes as a testament to her brilliant scheming, the rest of us are terrified she'll feel the need to interfere anytime we are the least bit unsettled. I went to great lengths to hide my breakup with Drew for fear she'd resurrect the dating game she played last Christmas. Uncle Michael hasn't been home for a visit since then, as he is the last unwed sibling and is horrified at the thought of what Nonna would do to find him the perfect husband.

The back door bangs open and Aunt Maggie Mae rushes through with the Evil Joes right behind her, followed by Uncle Marcus and the younger twins, Frankie and Freddie. Mary Jo and Jo Lynn are dressed in matching linen dresses, one in pale pink and the other in pale purple, their dark hair straight and slick, as if they are immune to the humidity.

Charlie does a quick sweep of the table and I can see the second it occurs to him where the only empty chairs are.

He leans close. "Switch with me." Charlie started calling our twin cousins Mary Jo and Jo Lynn the "Evil Joes" when we were twelve and they pulled a prank on him in Florida in front of some cute girls. Honestly, he was a little old to still be wearing *Star Wars* briefs. But because he was a member of the Fab Four with Sophie, Wes, and me, we had to back him up.

And Charlie is right—Evil Joes are evil.

I shake my head and grip the edges of my chair in case he decides to push me out. "Not happening."

"There's a guy with them," Wes whispers from across the table.

We all swivel toward where Aunt Maggie Mae and Uncle Marcus are sitting across the room, but I can't see who is with them because Uncle Ronnie is in the way.

"Is it one of the boyfriends?" I ask even though I know it's not, since Wes would recognize them. Aiden and Brent, the Joes' boyfriends, were invited to this but declined. That was a very stressful moment in the group text because very few people tell Nonna no.

Uncle Ronnie moves closer to Aunt Patrice, finally revealing the stranger in our midst.

The unknown guy standing next to Aunt Maggie Mae is tall with dark hair that sticks out in big, fat curls. He's wearing a faded tee and an even more faded pair of jeans that hang a little loose on his hips. He looks like he belongs hiking up a trail somewhere or maybe catching some waves or anywhere outdoors. He absolutely does not look comfortable in this crowded kitchen, wedged between my aunt and uncle.

He scans the room and I feel it when his attention lands on me. There's just a hint of a smile on his face, and I swear I know him. My mind is shuffling through the alphabet, testing out names beginning with each letter, hoping something pops.

I've got nothing.

Mary Jo drops down beside Charlie, her paper fluttering to rest on the table, and snatches his pencil.

Charlie lets out a loud breath, then reaches for one of the pencils in the center of the table he earlier deemed inferior.

"All right, everyone is here!" Nonna exclaims. "And I think this is by far the most graduates we've ever had at one time!"

My family is huge. And loud. My grandfather was born and raised in Sicily, but he met my grandmother while he was studying here. He was only supposed to stay in the US for a year, but they fell in love, got married, and had eight kids. He never went back to Sicily. Well, except for vacations. They celebrated their fiftieth wedding anniversary a few months ago. The same party where Aunt Patrice and Uncle Ronnie danced like no one was watching even though *everyone* was watching. They're both a little odd. Nonna and Papa = couple goals. Aunt Patrice and Uncle Ronnie? Not so much.

There are six of us graduating this year: Charlie, Sophie, Wes, the Evil Joes, and me. I glance down the table, where Wes sticks out as the only blond in the sea of dark hair. Wes has lived next door to Nonna and Papa his entire life and grew up with us. There are also over twenty members of the Messina family packed into the kitchen—aunts and uncles and cousins—some who have gone through this before us and others who will follow us. Oh, and one stranger.

I take one more peek at the guy next to Aunt Maggie Mae.

He's leaning against the far wall, arms crossed in front of him. He catches me staring, so I quickly swivel back around, embarrassed I got busted.

Nonna gets everyone's attention. "Okay, let's get started."

Jo Lynn sits up a little taller in her chair and looks toward her parents. "You want to do this with us?" she asks the guy I'm trying really hard not to look at. Maybe she's trying to make up for their boyfriends snubbing us?

Nonna shuffles around until she's almost backward in her chair. "Oh! Who's this?" she asks excitedly. "Yes, come join us!" she adds without even waiting for an answer.

Aunt Maggie Mae throws her arm around New Guy. "You remember Leo! Caroline and Alonso Perez's oldest?" Since he's now anchored to her side, it's easy for her to push him forward slightly so she can show him off to the room.

Leo Perez.

"Oh," Sophie says.

Charlie mutters something under his breath that would probably make Nonna reach for the nearest bar of soap.

Now the entire room has noticed him, and several family members welcome him to the chaos. The noise level inches up and up as it's prone to do when we're all crammed into one room. He's shaking hands and answering questions about his parents and what's going on with him, but I'm too far away to pick up what he's saying.

Of course it's Leo. But I didn't recognize him with his hair long and curly like that. He always kept it buzzed close to his head when we were kids. His face has lost its chubbiness, and he's grown at least a foot.

The Perez family lived next door to the Evil Joes until Mr. Perez got transferred right before we started eighth grade. Leo's parents were really close to Aunt Maggie Mae and Uncle Marcus. Their kids were inseparable, and they vacationed together in the summer. We always knew the Evil Joes would rather be with them than with us.

"Leo," Nonna says. "Jo Lynn is right; would you like to join us? You're graduating this year, too! You can tell us all about your plans."

Mary Jo scoots her chair over and says, "You can squeeze in right here." She nods to indicate the space between her and Jo Lynn.

For every inch Mary Jo moved closer to Charlie, Charlie has now moved closer to me.

Even though Leo's been around us in the past, it's been a long time and this group can be overwhelming. From the look on his face, I'm sure he doesn't remember all of our names or who goes with who, and it's easy to feel like at any moment there will be a quiz.

"I, uh, no thank you," Leo finally says.

Charlie lets out a grunt.

I whisper to Charlie, "It's been years. Let it go."

He gives me a funny look. "I'm good."

Charlie and Leo did not part on great terms. I think the last time they saw each other was at the park for the end-of-year party and Charlie was being obnoxious, just like every other seventh-grade boy. Charlie and his friend Judd were throwing a football and Charlie was running backward a little too fast trying to catch it and completely mowed over Jo Lynn. She stained her white jeans and started bawling. And because Leo was like a brother to them, he pushed Charlie before Charlie had a chance to apologize or help Jo Lynn up from the ground. So of course, Charlie pushed him back. I'm sure they think they had some super-masculine brawl, but it was really just a bunch of flailing arms and legs and near misses.

They both got sent home before the party was over.

And obviously, Charlie isn't over it.

"If you change your mind, feel free to jump right in," Nonna says, then spins back around in her chair. "Now, where were we?" Without looking behind her, she adds, "Dallas, if you sneak another piece of chicken from that tray, you're going to get it."

He lets out a squeak when his brother, Denver, elbows him in the stomach, only because Dallas has now ruined any chance of him snatching one, too. I feel for them. The smells that waft through Nonna's kitchen are enough to tempt even the most innocent into thievery. Dallas and Denver belong to Aunt Patrice and Uncle Ronnie. Even though their parents are weird, the boys are pretty cool despite the fact they were named for the cities they were conceived in.

We all know she's bluffing, but Denver backs away from the food anyway. The only way she's been able to hold everyone hostage for this is because dinner won't be served until after we're done.

Nonna slips on her reading glasses and glances at a clean copy of the questionnaire she printed for herself earlier in the week. "Okay, first question. Who's going to college?" She examines each of us. "I think we have a full sweep this year!" Her enthusiasm is the only thing keeping this Thing going year after year.

We all raise a hand, then call out the letters *LSU* as we write the answer on the line marked *If yes, where?* A loud chorus of "Match" rumbles through the room.

I skim the paper and hope the food isn't cold by the time we finish. There are so many questions.

"Next!" Nonna says. "What is your major?"

Even though I want to shout out my answer to help move this thing along, I'll have to wait my turn since Nonna starts on the opposite side of the table.

"Sophie, what did you put down?"

Sophie clears her throat and says, "Nursing." Charlie's mom, Aunt Ayin, raises her hand and shouts, "Match!" Sophie beams and Nonna claps.

Did I mention Nonna makes all the wives and husbands

who marry into this family retroactively fill out one of these forms so they can join in the fun? Being in this family is not for the fainthearted.

Next is Wes. When he calls out, "Business," four uncles and two aunts holler, "Match!"

And so it goes until we get around the table and it's Charlie's turn.

He hesitates a second and every eye in the room is on him. There is a string of 3-D geometric drawings lining the right edge of his paper that are perfection in shape and size. School is not his thing and I know he struggles with his parents' expectation that he follow in their footsteps and choose a career in medicine. But he's never going to do that; he gets squeamish at the sight of blood. Charlie is one of those people who is going to do great in the real world if only he can just get there.

"Undecided," he says, and he has, by far, the most matches in the room.

"You have plenty of time to decide what you want to do!" Nonna waves a hand toward the room. "They all seem to have figured it out."

He grins, then starts scribbling a brick wall along the bottom of his page.

"Olivia's turn," Nonna says.

I'm the exact opposite of Charlie. I love school. Love my classes. I've already studied the course catalog for next fall and can't wait for orientation, when I'll make my schedule.

"I'm double majoring in accounting and political science with a minor in Spanish," I answer.

Both of my parents could have matched me with the accounting part, but they're out of town for work this week. It's hard to stand out in a family this size, so I'm pleased that the room remains silent.

Until Jo Lynn says, "That's a weird combo."

"Not at all," I say. "I want to go to law school and specialize in international tax law."

The Evil Joes exchange a look that I decipher as them thinking I'm snotty, but I just know what I want. I'm driven. And I'm tired of this being something that people think I need to apologize for.

Nonna pats my hand. "And you'll do great! Everyone knows how hard you work! I just can't believe someone beat you out of valedictorian."

"I'm happy to take the second spot," I say quickly. And mostly that's true, but a small part of me is frustrated to have come so close to graduating with the highest honor and fallen just a bit short.

Nonna turns back to Sophie, moving to the next question, but I'm distracted by the notification that just popped up on my phone. It's an e-mail from the vice principal of my school.

Dragging the phone from the table, I settle it on my leg and slide it open.

To: Oliva Perkins
From: Dwayne Spencer
Subject: Off-campus PE form

Miss Perkins,
It has come to our attention that my office has not
received the form required to show proof of completion
of your off-campus PE class. I remind you that it is up to
you to ensure you fulfill the necessary hours and return a
completed valid form. In order to allow you to graduate
with your class, we will need to have your signed form no
later than 8 a.m. on Monday, May 16th.

Sincerely,
D. Spencer

I read it twice to make sure I understand what it says.
The coach who ran our class said he would turn all the forms
in to the school. I guess mine got lost somehow—but is this
missing form holding my degree hostage? I'm the salutatorian
of our class. I have taken seven AP classes. The reason I even
took off-campus PE was because that was the only way I could
make my schedule work with all the other classes I wanted
on my transcript. My choices were golf or tennis, and even
though Charlie insisted that I wasn't coordinated enough for

either, I agreed with him that I would stink at tennis but I could handle golf since it involved less running.

Today is May 8th, so Mr. Spencer has given me a week from tomorrow to clear this up. *It's just a mistake, it's just a mistake,* I chant in my head.

"Olivia?" Nonna asks.

I snap to attention.

Charlie leans in close. "Favorite club," he whispers.

I draw a blank. The past four years fade away now that I can't think past the e-mail.

"It's probably same as mine," Charlie blurts out.

Tilting my head toward him, I glance at his paper.

Ping-Pong Club

I didn't even know we had one of those, but I nod and say, "Yes, so fun."

My eyes go back to Mr. Spencer's e-mail. My chest starts to feel tight and my breath comes a little quicker.

"Next question!" Nonna announces.

"We need to speed this along," Uncle Charles says. "Or we'll be eating this food for breakfast."

Uncle Marcus yells, "Match!"

Nonna looks at me, completely ignoring two of her sons. "Let's start with Olivia and go back around the opposite way this time."

I read the next question aloud. "Where do you see yourself living in ten years?"

In my head, my answer is: *In a cardboard box because I'm jobless and homeless because I never graduated high school.*

Taking a deep breath, I say, "Undecided."

A chorus of matches echoes through the room, even though almost everyone who says that ended up right back here in Shreveport, only a few blocks from this very house.

There are twenty more questions and I'm not sure I can face answering them in this room.

"I don't feel so good," I whisper, but it's loud enough for Nonna to hear.

Concern washes across her face. "What's wrong?"

I shrug. "Not sure. I feel sick."

Grabbing my paper, I push back from the table and weave through the crowd toward the back door.

"We lost one. Does that mean we're done and can eat?" Uncle Sal asks.

I'm racing down the driveway, but I stop short when I see someone on Nonna's front porch.

Leo.

He's sitting on the steps, looking at his phone, but stands when he sees me.

"You okay?" he asks.

I'm sure he can see the panic rolling off me like waves.

I shake my head and continue down the driveway. He jumps off the front steps and falls in line beside me.

"I didn't know anyone was out here," I say, hoping my voice sounds even and steady.

"It felt like I was intruding. I mean, I'm not even sure what's going on in there, but it seems like some family thing."

The two blocks of sidewalk between Nonna's house and mine feel more like a mile right now. I'm an inch from freaking all the way out and I really don't want to do that in front of Leo.

"Why'd you leave? It seems like there was probably another hour or so to go," Leo says, chuckling.

"Not feeling so good," I say. With my arms wrapped tightly around my waist, it's easy enough to believe.

"Oh," he says. "Do you need anything?"

I shake my head. "No. Just couldn't take the crowd."

He nods like he totally understands. Which I guess he does since he was hiding out on the front porch.

We stop in front of my house. "Thanks for walking me home," I say. It's been years since I've seen him and I should make some effort to ask how he's been or what he's been up to, but my brain has that e-mail scrolling on repeat.

"Sure," he says, then points back to Nonna's house. "I'll just head back now."

It's awkward. For both of us.

I turn and walk up the front path to my house.

Leo calls out, "Hope you feel better," just as I'm opening my front door.

I give him a small smile and wave before disappearing inside.

My phone is buzzing with texts from Charlie, Sophie, and Wes in our group chat. I message back I'm fine just need a minute to stop them from following me here.

After I race up the stairs to my room, it only takes a few seconds to grab the blank copy of the form I gave my golf instructor at the beginning of the semester. There are boxes that Coach was supposed to check stating that either we *did* or *did not* complete the required hours of instruction. I clearly remember him stating at the beginning of the semester that he would turn in the forms to the school directly so that the students couldn't alter them in any way.

Pulling my phone back out, I shoot a reply to Mr. Spencer.

To: Dwayne Spencer
From: Olivia Perkins
Subject: Re: Off-campus PE form

Mr. Spencer,
There must be some mistake. I finished the class. Coach Cantu told us at the beginning of the semester that he turns the forms in directly to you. There shouldn't be any reason why you don't have mine.

I will contact Coach Cantu to find out what happened. In a
worst-case scenario—I really don't think this is possible but
I'm trying not to freak out—what happens if he won't sign
it for some insane reason? Would this really stop me from
graduating?

Sincerely,
Olivia Perkins

I refresh my e-mail over and over. And over. It's fifteen
minutes before I get his reply.

To: Oliva Perkins
From: Dwayne Spencer
Subject: Re: Off-campus PE form

Miss Perkins,
If you are unable to turn in a signed form stating you
have met the requirements for the class, you will be short
of what the state requires for you to graduate. Since we
are a public institution, I would be unable to make any
exceptions. This is the risk you run when you decide to take
a class off-campus.

Sincerely,
D. Spencer

God, could he be any colder? And now I'm really panicking. It's only seconds before I'm pulling my car out into the street, headed for the public golf course nestled deep in the middle of an old neighborhood not far from mine where our class met on Tuesdays and Thursdays during the semester.

The sky is crystal blue and we're in that really small patch of time where it's warm out but the humidity doesn't feel like you've walked into a wet, hot blanket. So it's no surprise the parking lot is completely full. For the next couple of weeks, this place will stay packed from sunup to sundown.

This course has seen better days, but it is well loved for its location. All the newer, fancier courses, especially the one that was completed last year right outside of town, require a hefty membership and certain social standing to feel comfortable.

This one is as low-key as it gets.

I pull in the back where the employees park, since I'll only be here a few minutes.

There's a groundskeeper in the small garage where old golf carts go to die. He's piling landscaping tools into a trailer attached to one of those side-by-side vehicles. The smell of gasoline and freshly cut grass permeates the air, and the patch on his grease-stained uniform says *Mitch*.

"Excuse me, I'm looking for Coach Cantu?"

The man's brow creases like he doesn't know who I'm asking for.

"The golf pro here. Coach Cantu," I repeat.

Mitch's face lights up. "Oh, you mean John! Yeah, he's not here," he says, then turns his back to me to grab another piece of handheld equipment.

I try to swallow down my frustration. "Do you know when he will be back?"

Mitch stops and looks up as if the answer is somehow written on the cobwebbed ceiling. "Well, I think he's gone."

"Gone? What do you mean, gone?" I can't keep the panic from crawling into my voice.

"He doesn't work here anymore. We had a cake on Friday to say our good-byes. Chocolate."

The floor is sucking me in. "Do you know where he went? Is he still in town?"

"Maybe check with Susie. She probably knows." He tilts his head toward the front office, shrugs, and gets back to work.

I race inside and make a beeline for the woman at the counter, prepared to do whatever I have to so I can get a clear answer when I repeat the same questions to her.

Susie flinches as if in pain. "I'm right here. No need to yell. He's the pro at Ellerbe Hills now. Not sure when he's starting over there, though."

"Can you give me his number?" It feels like my knees are about to give out.

She's shaking her head. "Sorry, I can't give out employees' numbers."

"But you said he's not an employee here anymore."

By her look, she doesn't appreciate the reminder. "But he *was*."

We stare at each other long enough for it to be clear she's not budging, so I leave and walk numbly back to my car.

I'm sitting at the kitchen table, staring out the window that looks onto the driveway and the side of the neighbor's house.

The house is quiet. Empty. And for the first time, I don't like it.

My parents were hired to swoop into a large corporation's New Orleans office for a surprise audit and it's expected to take them all week to get it done. I made a deal with them that I would get Life360 on my phone so I could stay here alone while they are out of town instead of two blocks over at Nonna's, and now I'm regretting it a little. In the quiet, there's nothing to distract my brain from rolling over and over the same thing—what if I don't graduate? But I'm also glad Mom isn't here because there's no way I wouldn't blurt out everything in one giant breath. And I'm not ready for her to know just yet.

Because if she knows, my grandparents know. And if my grandparents know, then all my aunts and uncles know. And instead of being Olivia, the one who always has everything together and will conquer the world, I'll forever be Olivia, the one who might lose out on graduating as salutatorian, all because of a dumb off-campus PE golf class. All the other things I've accomplished will be overshadowed by this one thing, and I can't go down like that.

I am going to fix this without my parents ever knowing.

I could call my brother, Jake, but I'm not sure what he can do. He's not even coming home this summer, except for my graduation day. Jake and our cousin Graham took jobs in Gulf Shores, where they spend every morning hauling chairs and umbrellas out to the beach and then spend every evening packing them back up. I think they plan on ending the summer with a good tan and a pocketful of tip money.

My phone vibrates on the table, startling me.

MOM: The questionnaire seemed to go faster this year! I'm surprised since there are so many of y'all graduating. I saw you went to the golf course but didn't stay very long. Dad was hoping you developed a love for the game!

I let out a sigh. Ever since I agreed to Life360 on my phone, Mom's new favorite pastime is watching my every move. She even has those parameters set up that send an alert when I either come home or leave. And it's not like she's trying to catch me doing something wrong. . . . I think she's genuinely fascinated by being able to see my every move. I mean, I can't pass the grocery store without her texting me to pick up milk or any other item she thinks I need while she's gone.

ME: I thought I left my sweater there but they didn't have it
MOM: Oh, okay. The blue one? I thought I saw that in your closet. I hope you haven't lost the soft pink one. It looks so good on you.
MOM: Say a prayer to St. Anthony. $5.00. It will turn up.

My mother's answer for every lost item—pray to St. Anthony and offer up a monetary reward for the poor box at church. In her mind it's foolproof.

ME: Yes Ma'am

I put my phone down again and open up my laptop, searching for e-mails from Coach that he sent throughout the semester. Maybe I can contact him that way. I find one he sent from his school account and hit REPLY.

Coach Cantu,
Hello. This is Olivia Perkins and I believe there has been a mistake with my off-campus PE form. The school office never received it. I'm happy to bring you a copy at your

earliest convenience! Please let me know the best time and place.

Thank you so much,
Olivia Perkins

I hit SEND and stare at my in-box, willing his reply to be instantaneous. But it's not. So I start a group text with a few friends who took his class with me.

ME: hey trying to get in touch with Coach Cantu but all I have is his school e-mail. Anyone have his number?

At least the replies come in pretty quick.

STEWART: No only e-mail
BRIDGET: Sorry! I don't!
HECTOR: Have you tried to call the golf course?
CASSIE: Uggghhh so glad that class is over! I hate golf! Why do you want to talk to him????
ME: Need to get a copy of my form. The office misplaced mine.

Okay, so a little white lie. Also, trying to feel them out to see if they heard from our vice principal, too.

BRIDGET: Oh! I'm so sorry! He'll sign it for you again. He's the nicest guy!

HECTOR: Cassie we all know you hate golf. You told us every chance you got

CASSIE: I wouldn't hate it if they let us use the carts. Why would I want to carry that bag all over the course when there are carts?!

I reply with a quick thanks! and exit out of the conversation even though it's still going. I'm desperate when I pull up social media thinking I can send him a DM, but my searches come up empty. So I open up the browser, putting *Ellerbe Hills Country Club* into the search engine, and scan the results. The club name, address, and phone number pop up right above an article about when the land was purchased and what the timeline for construction would be from a few years ago. Coach Cantu is moving up in the world if he's the golf pro at the newest golf course in this area.

I call them and cross my fingers I can get him on the phone.

"Ellerbe Hills Country Club," a woman says.

"Hi, yes, um, I'm looking for Coach Cantu?"

Before I can ask anything else, she says, "This line is for the clubhouse. If you're looking for a player or coach, you need to call them directly." And then the line goes dead.

I shake my phone in the air as if that will do any good. "But I don't know how to contact him directly," I bite out.

I pull up the club's website to check their hours and realize that by the time I could get there, they would be closing for the day.

Tomorrow.

I'll drive out there tomorrow.

An e-mail notification pops up and it's a response from Coach. Thankfully, I'm alone in the house, so no one comes running when I let out a massive squeal.

I open it up.

Thank you for your e-mail. After May 5th, I will be unavailable for the summer. If you have an immediate concern, please contact Vice Principal Spencer.

Thanks!
Coach Cantu

It's a flipping automatic out-of-office reply. Directing me to the one person I don't want to talk to right now.

This is great. Just great.

I'll just have to go there tomorrow. Once I find him, he'll sign my form. Then I'll hand-deliver it to Mr. Spencer to ensure it doesn't get lost a second time. There is no alternative.

And then I get another text from Mom.

MOM: Can't wait to hear about Bailey's party tomorrow. Rhonda bumped into Tiffany at the florist this morning and Kyle from Colony House did the flowers. She said they are OVER THE TOP so you know I'm going to need pictures. Lots of pics!

I glance at the wall across from me. There is a line of graduation party invitations hanging by clothespins to a piece of twine that Mom stretched out between the fridge and the pantry door.

How could I forget it's Senior Party Week? I've literally been waiting for this week for the past four years.

Senior Party Week is the week between the end of finals and graduation. We're done with school, but not officially, so this dead week is filled with parties to help pass the time. I'm not sure when or how the tradition started, but it's out of control. Just like the questionnaire, these parties are *A Thing*. They're given by friends and family of graduating seniors to honor them—all with a theme. And each year the themes get more and more extravagant. Not every senior is thrown a party, but there's a good chance every senior is invited to at least one per day. Sometimes two.

I don't think it's normal to have so many graduation parties and I'm not sure anywhere else does it like we do, but if we're going to be weird about something, I'm glad this is it.

My family is throwing a big crawfish boil Friday night honoring the six of us who are graduating, so we're part of the madness. I can remember looking at posts on social media over the last three years from the seniors ahead of me and feeling like I could not wait for my turn.

I pluck the invitation for Bailey's party from the twine. It's pink and purple and in big letters across the top it says *PJs and Pancakes!* It starts at nine thirty a.m. and we're supposed to show up in our pajamas. Bailey is a good friend, and for about thirty seconds, I consider waiting to find Coach until after the party, but I'm not sure how I'll even get through the night with this hanging over me, much less be able to push it off until after lunch. So I think through how I can take care of this golf business before the party. I'll need to get to the country club first thing in the morning, handle this with Coach, then get back here to change into my pj's before going to the party. I can drop the form off to Mr. Spencer after that.

No biggie. I got this.

My phone buzzes again.

MOM: Don't forget to pick up Bailey's gift. I'll send you the address. It should be wrapped and ready, you'll just need to sign the card. Just make sure you leave with enough time to be there when the store opens since the party is so early. You don't want to be late!

Great. For one second I forgot about Mom tracking me. There will be questions. So many questions as to why I'm driving way out to Ellerbe Hills, since I know she'll be on the lookout for me making the party on time.

The side door bangs open and I hear Charlie holler, "I know you're faking. You just didn't want to fill out that form."

He comes into the kitchen and goes straight to the fridge, like always.

"It was awful, O. Evil Joes laughed at every single one of my answers. Every. Single. One. Even if they matched." He pulls out cheese, lunch meat, mayo, lettuce, and spicy mustard. Then he heads to the pantry for the bread. "I mean, how can they laugh when we have the same answer?" He stops what he's doing and spins around to face me. "The same exact answer."

"Because they're evil?" I offer.

He waves the mustard bottle at me. "That is correct. They are evil." And then he's back to digging through the fridge.

"Didn't you eat at Nonna's?" I ask.

"No. I left as soon as we finished the questionnaire. Told them I needed to check on you. Couldn't take the Joes a minute longer. So now I'm starving."

I glance at the clock on the oven. "It's just now over?" I went to find Coach and made it back home and they were still answering questions?

"It's just now over. From this moment on, no matter what's going on in my life, I will be out of town when it comes time to fill out the questionnaire."

"It was weird Leo was there, right? Did you find out why he's in town?" I ask. Maybe that came up after I left.

Charlie shrugs. "No idea. Don't care." While he builds his sandwich, I rack my brain on how to make it to Ellerbe Hills and back, get to the store to pick up Bailey's gift, then get to the party by nine thirty. In. The. Morning.

Without Mom knowing what I'm doing.

Maybe I could just leave my phone. Maybe that's the best choice. But what if it takes longer at the course than I think it will? And I know Mom will be blowing me up about what I'm wearing to the party.

A chair screeches against the floor as Charlie settles in at the table with his plate and takes a huge bite of his sandwich.

Charlie. Charlie is the answer.

"Truth or dare?" I ask him, and he freezes, his cheeks puffed out full of food.

I've pulled out the big guns and he knows it.

"What do you want?" he asks once he's swallowed down his bite, completely ignoring my question.

"Truth or dare?" I hope I can get him to agree to help me regardless of the choice he makes.

Charlie puts the sandwich down and slowly wipes his mouth. This is a game we've played for years, and he and I take it very seriously. More seriously than Wes and Sophie, who always find ways around the dares and are happy with half-truths. Charlie and I are purists when it comes to truth or dare. You have to pick one and you have to follow through.

Please pick dare. . . . Please pick dare. . . .

"You were freaking out at Nonna's, so I know something's up. I'm guessing whatever brought this up has something to do with that. So, since that scares the crap out of me, I'm going with truth."

Dang. A dare would have been a sure thing. Now I'll have to improvise.

I clear my throat, and he pushes his plate to the side even though he's barely eaten.

"I have a problem. A big one."

Charlie nods, giving me all the encouragement I need.

"You know how I still needed half a credit of PE at the beginning of this semester, but I also wanted to take that law studies class?"

"So you took golf off-campus. I know. What's the problem?"

I lean back in my chair and tilt my head to look up at the ceiling. I don't want to see his reaction when I tell him.

"Well, Coach Cantu didn't turn in my form. I got an e-mail from Mr. Spencer today that says if I don't turn in the completed form by next Monday, then I won't graduate."

Charlie starts laughing. Like, really laughing. Just like I knew he would. "I told you golf would be a disaster!"

I glare at him. "Now is not the time for *I told you so.*"

"This is the exact perfect time for *I told you so*. Never, ever has there been a time when *I told you so* was more needed. Because I literally said *Don't take off-campus PE. It will be a disaster.*" He holds his hands out toward me. "And see? Disaster."

I throw my pen at him.

He dodges it easily; the grin persists. "What's this got to do with truth or dare?"

I take a deep breath and say, "I need to go to Ellerbe Hills Country Club and find Coach Cantu and beg him to sign my form so I can turn it in but I can't do that while Mom is tracking my every move since I also have to pick up the gift for Bailey's party then be at her party by nine thirty in the morning so I need someone to switch phones and *be me* in the morning and will you be that person? That's the question I need you to answer."

Charlie rolls his eyes. "This is the dumbest use of truth or dare I've ever seen. You should be ashamed."

"Add that to the list, then," I say. "I was hoping you'd go for dare."

"I figured. Why don't you find him after the party?" Charlie asks.

"There's no way I will enjoy Bailey's party if all I'm thinking about is if there's a chance I really might not graduate. Plus, I need you to man my phone regardless of when I go so I don't have twenty questions from Mom." I don't tell Charlie, but ever since I got the e-mail from Mr. Spencer, I feel like I have a black cloud hanging over me. This is supposed to be the best week of high school! Nothing but parties and fun and friends. I need this settled. I need to know this is not a problem.

Charlie leans closer to the table and I mirror his movement. "I should say no on principle since you've abused truth or dare."

"I'm desperate."

He rolls his eyes again, then sits back, pulling his plate in front of him so he can take another big bite. Forcing me to wait for his answer.

While he swallows, he gives me *a look*. "Will you admit I was right and golf turned out to be a total disaster?"

"Yes, if that's what it takes for you to agree."

Charlie keeps demolishing his sandwich, but I can tell I've got him. He dips his thumb in a stray blob of mustard on the plate. "I mean, how can I say no to this? But I know there's more to it if you brought in truth or dare."

"There's really not. He's going to sign it and it will be done and over."

He shrugs. "Yeah, sure, I'll be you."

I jump up from my seat and rush around to his side of the table, throwing my arms around his neck. "Thank you! Thank you!"

"I have to answer texts from Aunt Lisa, huh?"

"Yes! That's it! Answer like you're me." I don't add that she texts a lot. He'll figure that out.

The side door opens, and Wes and Sophie come in laughing, hand in hand. Sophie's eyes land on mine. "Are you okay?" she asks.

Before I can open my mouth, Charlie answers. "Oh, she's fine. Just freaking out because she may not graduate."

So maybe Nonna isn't the only bigmouth in the family.

Wes and Sophie drop down at the table with us.

"What do you mean?" Wes asks. "You're like the runner-up!"

"Salutatorian," I correct him.

He shakes his head. "Same thing."

"So, if the valedictorian can't perform their duties, does the crown pass to you?" Charlie asks.

I give them both the stink eye.

Sophie shoves Charlie for me, since she's closer. "Catch us up, Olivia. What happened?"

I tell them the short version, and the first thing Wes says is "I knew golf was a bad idea."

Charlie holds his hand up for Wes to high-five him, both of them finding amusement at my expense. Thankfully, Sophie turns to her other side and gives Wes a good shove, too, then changes the subject.

"Oh! Nonna started talking about the party for all of us on Friday night," Sophie says with a horrified expression.

"And mentioned we should all dress in matching clothes—you know, like we do at Christmas?"

We all cringe. In October or November every year, Nonna picks out a pajama design so we're all matchy-matchy on Christmas morning. But no one should see Uncle Ronnie in those tight-fitting onesies he favors, no matter how cute the print is.

"Nonna thinks just because one of her crazy plans worked out that she's unstoppable now," I say, then nod toward Sophie and Wes. "I mean, things did work out for y'all, but we had to wade through a lot of bad to get there."

No one could forget some of the weirder dates Sophie had to go on.

Wes shakes his head, chuckling. "She had that look. You know the one I mean."

"And she's *requested* all family be close by for the weekend through both graduation ceremonies. Mine is the day before y'all's," Sophie says. "That's going to be a lot of family dinners."

We talk into the night as if we haven't all been together this entire weekend. Just after eleven, Charlie and Wes get ready to head to Wes's house, where they'll stay the night. Sophie has to drive home, since she has graduation practice at her school first thing in the morning.

She walks Wes out, her hand anchored in his, and I see that Charlie has learned from experience to give them a few minutes to say their good-byes.

I'm cleaning up the few dishes and putting away snacks when I say, "Don't forget to be here at eight in the morning. I want to get out there and back as early as possible."

"That'll work. You can get it done before your mom starts texting."

I nod but don't say anything. Charlie hands me the last glass, and he can tell something's up. "I mean, she won't start texting at eight in the morning, will she?"

I shrug and give him an *I don't think so* look.

He lets out a groan. "You better be quick," he says, then throws open the door. Wes and Sophie almost tumble back inside since he apparently had her pressed against it for their good-night kiss.

"Y'all are killing me," Charlie says as he bounces down the steps.

Sophie buries her face in Wes's neck and he whispers in her ear. She's giggling. I'm super happy for them, but it is a little hard to watch sometimes.

And I'm not too proud to admit I'm a tiny bit jealous. When my relationship ended with my ex-boyfriend, Drew, I didn't tell anyone in the family besides the Fab Four until months later, scared that Nonna would pull the same stunt on me that she did with Sophie. I mean, she did try, but it had been so long since I was any kind of upset about the breakup that it never turned into anything, thank God.

Finally, Sophie and Wes part ways and they both tell me

good night as he walks her to her car. I turn off all the lights and head upstairs, going through my nighttime rituals. Once I slide between the sheets, though, I can't get comfortable. I toss and turn for a long time, thinking about Coach Cantu and that stupid form. But by this time tomorrow, everything will be back on track.

PJS
and PANCAKES

Honoring
BAILEY THOMAS!

Monday, May 9th
9:30 am
Bailey's House!

Truth #2: There are good plans, and there are plans you make when you're desperate

Monday, May 9th, Morning

Olivia

Charlie showed up at 8:12 only after I called him three times and threatened to sic the Evil Joes on him if he didn't get down to my house pronto.

He was in his pj's, the ones from two Christmases ago that have Santa hat–wearing polar bears all over them. I've got a matching set upstairs. Charlie kept his eyes open long enough for us to trade phones and passwords before he fell onto the couch in the den and was back asleep.

Following the directions from Maps, twenty-five minutes later I'm finally pulling up to the gates of Ellerbe Hills Country Club.

Stopping at the guard station, I lower my window and give my friendliest smile. "Hi! I'm here to see Coach Cantu!"

Okay, so that was way too enthusiastic.

And by the look on the guard's face, he's not impressed.

"Club isn't open on Mondays."

And then he turns back around and disappears inside his little booth.

That's it? I can't wait until tomorrow. Another twenty-four hours of worrying and just—no. No, no, no.

I wave my hand and he begrudgingly emerges.

"I desperately need to find the coach for my school's team, who I heard works here now. I really need to talk to him. I don't know where else to look."

I mean, what if he's on vacation? Or I can't find him? Panic. Sheer panic at the possibility of not graduating because I can't locate Coach Cantu has melted my brain. I'm already terrified my family and friends will find out how bad I screwed this up as it is. School is *my* thing. The Thing I'm really good at. If this gets out, it will be the *only thing* they remember from my high school career, the annual joke every Christmas dinner until the end of time. Not how I was awarded salutatorian. Not all the AP classes. Not the hours and hours of studying. It will be *Remember that time Olivia almost didn't graduate because she screwed up golf?* Four years whittled down to one sentence.

This will not be my legacy.

"Please help me," I beg him. My phone (or really, Charlie's phone) is ringing and I see my name flash across the screen. I mute the incoming call. I can't talk to him right now.

The guard blows out a long breath. "Look, there's no one here today but the groundskeepers. But I do know there's a big golf tournament this week for the high school kids. There will be staff setting up for it tomorrow and some of the teams have plans to play through. I have no idea if the guy you're looking for will be here. That's the best I can do."

I'm nodding and trying to take deep breaths to calm down. "Thank you," I say. "Thank you so much! I'll be back tomorrow!"

I've driven almost twenty minutes to find out no one is here. It will be a miracle if I get through the next twenty-four hours without losing it.

Phone Duty: Charlie

That noise. What is that noise? I reach for my covers so I can pull them over my head and it takes me a few grabs to realize there are no covers.

And there it is again.

I peel my eyes open and have no idea where I am. Or what

day it is. Then I catch a glimpse of that awful bird sculpture Uncle Bruce bought at some auction and I remember I'm at Olivia's on her couch.

Why am I at Olivia's?

And why is my phone blowing up?

Thoughts of golf and her phone and Aunt Lisa hit me all at once. I feel around for the phone on the floor next to the couch. It's one of those obnoxious oversize ones that doesn't allow you to do anything on it with one hand. It's like texting on a tablet. I tap in the code Olivia told me. For someone as smart she is, I'm not gonna lie, I expected a better password than her birthday. It takes my eyes a few seconds to adjust to the screen.

MOM: Good morning, sweetie!

MOM: Reminding you about Bailey's gift! It's an adorable pair of monogrammed slippers for the dorm. Thought that was a perfect gift for a PJ party! The store opens at 9 so you probably need to be there right when the door opens so you're not late for the party.

MOM: Don't forget to sign the card

MOM: What pjs are you going to wear? Those PJ Harlow ones you got for Christmas would be super cute. Make sure to wear a cute sports bra underneath it because I think those arm holes gape a bit.

I fling Olivia's phone back on the floor. What the hell. She's barely been gone five minutes and I'm already going to have to talk to Aunt Lisa? About bras?

I pick the phone back up, but instead of answering the texts, I call my number. It goes to voice mail. Did she decline my call?

Taking a deep breath, I read through Aunt Lisa's texts one more time, trying to come up with a good reply that saves me from having to discuss underwear. Can I just say *Okay!* to all of that? I scroll up to earlier conversations between Olivia and Aunt Lisa, and while it's good to see Olivia doesn't text nearly as much as her mom, she rarely answers with a simple *Okay!*

She did not prepare me for this.

And oh Lord, here comes another one.

MOM: And since those bottoms are silk, watch the panty lines too

Okay, this has gone too far. Too. Far.

I call Sophie, the only other person who can help me with this, because God forbid Aunt Lisa decides to call Olivia if she's not responding quick enough.

She answers on the second ring. "I'm at grad rehearsal," she whispers. "Can't talk right now."

And then she hangs up.

They're both getting it when I see them next. Finally, my name pops up on the screen. Olivia is calling me back.

"Hey," Olivia says when I answer. "What's up?"

"Your mom. Already texting me. I'm sending you a screen-shot."

I wait until I hear that swooshing sound and then Olivia starts laughing. "Tell her this exactly: I'm wearing the pj's Sophie gave me, so I'm all good."

I put Olivia on speaker so I can respond to her mom and talk at the same time. "I didn't sign up for this," I say.

"Yes, you did. This is being me."

"Oh God, Aunt Lisa is texting back."

I watch those three little dots jump around forever and worry about the length and subject matter of the next text.

MOM: Oh good! That will look fantastic with your tan. Are you wearing your hair down? Or maybe two braids. That would be precious.

"This is not happening," I say to Olivia, then recite Aunt Lisa's message to her. "Is she always like this?"

"Yep. And just reply: *Down.*"

I do as she says. "Is she going to ask for a selfie of you dressed up like this? Because I'm not sure I can be you to that extent."

"Ha! No. She asked me for a selfie a few years ago and then she posted it on Facebook with some sappy caption and now she knows she's banned from getting selfies of me forever. She likes to ramble but doesn't expect much in return."

"I get why you pulled out the truth or dare."

"I'm on my way back. Today was a bust. The club isn't open, which I totally didn't notice when I looked up their hours yesterday. I don't usually screw the details up like this." Olivia mumbles the last part. She's so used to being on top of everything that she's really hard on herself the few times she messes up. I know how bad this whole thing is screwing with her.

"But I still need you to go grab that gift if you can. I'll meet you in front of Bailey's house at nine thirty. I brought the pj's with me just in case."

"Send me the location," I say, and end the call. Hopefully I can get there and back before Aunt Lisa texts again.

Since my truck is still in front of Wes's house, I jog back down that way. I have my hand on the door but look toward my grandparents' house. I bet there's food there. And just the thought of that has my stomach rumbling.

Checking the time on Olivia's phone, I see I've got a few minutes to spare, so I run across the yard, clearing the back-porch steps in one leap.

The smell of bacon slams into me as soon as I open the door—just like it's supposed to. God, I love bacon.

"Good morning!" I yell as I walk into the back of the house.

Nonna peeks her head out of the kitchen and smiles when she sees me. "Good morning! Want some breakfast?"

"Does the Pope wear a funny hat?"

She chuckles as I follow her to the stove. "Make a plate. There's bacon and biscuits. Let me know if you want eggs."

I grab a quick hug from her, then head to the cabinet. "You're making my day, Nonna."

The doorbell rings and we both look toward the front of the house. No one rings the bell. Ever.

"Let me see who that is," she says before leaving the room.

I pile a huge amount of bacon on my plate and two biscuits. The jelly and butter are already out, so I slather some of both on each one. Just as I'm sitting down, I hear Nonna heading back this way.

"Leo, would you like some breakfast?"

I freeze as he enters the kitchen, waiting for the Evil Joes to show, but it's just him.

"No, thanks. I just ate," he says to Nonna, then nods to me. "Hey."

"What's up," I say. He's obviously just showered, since his hair is still wet and he's wearing nice clothes. Like ones that have been ironed. At eight forty-five in the morning. What's wrong with this guy?

"What brings you here?" I hear the tone as soon as the

words leave my mouth. From his flinch, he didn't miss it either. I feel bad for a split second until I remember he actually likes the Evil Joes.

"Mae sent me over to grab a bag she left here last night."

Mae. He calls her Mae?

Nonna waves a hand around. "I know just the one you mean. Found it last night after everyone left but didn't know whose it was. Let me go get it."

She steps out of the room and I turn my back to him, digging into my food.

"How long are you in town?" I ask, still not looking at him.

"The week," he answers.

God, why would you want to stay a week with Aunt Maggie Mae?

"It's not that bad," he says, defensively, and I realize I asked that question out loud. Whoops.

Thankfully, Nonna's back. "Here it is," she says. "Are you sure you don't want some food?"

It's a nearly impossible feat to visit this house and leave without consuming something.

"Yes, ma'am, I'm sure. But thank you," he says. And then to me: "See you later, Charlie."

I raise one hand and answer, "Yeah. See you around."

I'm washing my dish when Nonna gets back from walking Leo to the door. "He's such a nice young man," she says.

I tilt my head and shrug. "Yeah, I guess." I give her a loud kiss on the cheek. "Thanks for the fill-up." And then I'm out of there.

I've got twenty minutes to get to that store, grab the gift, then get to Bailey's house.

The store is in one of those glass-front strips. Parking in the closest spot I can find, I dash to the front door and arrive just as a girl in her twenties is unlocking it.

She pulls the door open and eyes me up and down, clearly trying hard to keep a straight face.

It's the first moment I realize I'm still in the pj bottoms and T-shirt I slept in.

"Oh, uh, yeah, I'm here to pick up a gift my aunt ordered. Lisa Perkins."

"Sure thing. Right this way," she says, and leads me to the counter in the back of the store. The metal shelves behind the register are stacked full of gifts. It takes her a minute to locate the one Aunt Lisa ordered.

"Are those grad gifts?" I ask.

"Yes! Graduation and Christmas are our busiest times of the year," she answers.

Seems like a racket. But whatever.

She pushes a ledger in front of me and I sign for the gift, then run back out to my truck. Just as I'm cranking the engine, there's another text from Aunt Lisa.

MOM: Oh good! You got the gift! Send me a pic of it so I can see how they wrapped it.

What. The. Actual . . . She wants a pic of a present? And it's no joke what Olivia said. Aunt Lisa probably tracked this phone all the way to the store. There's no way the trip to the golf course would have gone unnoticed.

Trying to figure out where to put the present for the pic without giving away that this is not Olivia's car, I end up stepping back outside and putting the gift on the hood. I frame the shot so that the store is in the background and I cut the image off at the bottom edge so she can't see the color of my truck. I snap the pic and send it to her.

And then I haul it to Bailey's before another text can come through.

Olivia

I get to Bailey's before Charlie. Crawling into the backseat, I'm thankful for my tinted windows as I change quickly into the pj's I'd stashed here this morning. The simple short-sleeve tee and shorts have become my favorite set since Sophie gave them to me a few months ago, and it shows from their frayed edges and slightly faded mint-green color.

Once I'm dressed, I take a few minutes for some deep breaths. I want to enjoy Bailey's party without this golf catastrophe hanging over me. I inhale and hold my breath for ten seconds, then let it out slowly, repeating several times.

Charlie pulls up just as I'm climbing back into the front seat. He parks in front of me and we meet in between our two vehicles.

He's got a small wrapped package in one hand and a plain white card in the other. "Your mom has texted three times reminding you to sign the card." Charlie hands me the gift and then holds up three fingers. "Three times."

I nod. "You know how she is," I say.

He's shaking his head. "Yeah, I don't know how she is. My aunt Lisa is cool. Laid-back. One of my favorites. I don't know who this monster is."

I lean closer to him and get a sniff. "You stopped at Nonna's for breakfast first, didn't you? You smell like bacon."

"I could practically taste it from Wes's driveway. It calls to me and I can't deny it."

"So you had time for breakfast but not enough time to change? You'll be the only guy here, but you should come on in, since you're dressed for the party," I say, motioning to the pj's he's still wearing.

He pops up a little straighter and looks toward Bailey's. Charlie couldn't care less about being the sole guy at a girls-only party. "I could totally do a second breakfast." Then he turns back to me. "Speaking of being dressed up, guess who showed up at Nonna's?"

"Um, it would take me ten minutes to go through the list of our family members."

His lips flatten into a line. "Not family. It was Leo. It's weird he's here."

I'm trying to figure out how being dressed up made him think of Leo, but it's Charlie and he probably doesn't even know how he made that leap.

"I bet he got invited to some of the nighttime parties. I'm sure he's kept in touch with his old friends, not just the Evil Joes," I say, and by Charlie's expression, I realize he's never thought that was a possibility.

"I don't care where he shows up, but *you* know he's on *their* side. Might as well call him Jo-Leo."

"Or Leo-Jo," I add, and we both laugh.

"We should be surprised you're here, Charlie, but we're not!"

His shoulders stiffen as we both recognize the voice.

"Evil Joes are here?" he whispers. "It's like we've summoned them."

"Bailey invited a big group to this," I answer.

My friend group is complicated. Charlie and Wes are my best friends at school, but I'm also close to a small group of girls, including Bailey, Mia, Bianca, and Danlee. But those girls cross over into other groups, like Bailey and her soccer friends, Mia and her drama club friends, and Bianca and her friends on the yearbook staff. Danlee is considered a floater, since she gets along with everyone and maneuvers between groups easily. The Evil Joes play soccer with Bailey, so when our friend groups collide, I cross paths with my least favorite cousins more often than I'd like.

Charlie and I wait as long as we can before acknowledging the Joes. When they stop in front of us, both girls are looking him up and down.

"Christmas jammies are a brave choice," Jo Lynn says.

"Especially ones from two years ago," Mary Jo adds with an evil smirk. And they would know how old they are because, of course, they had a set just like this, too.

Charlie leans closer to me. "Do they look too small?" he asks.

My forehead scrunches up and I lift my shoulders. "Uh, maybe the pants are a little short?" And now I know he's having flashbacks of when the Joes locked him out of our condo at the beach and he was wearing nothing but underwear. Themed underwear that were a tad too tight.

Just before he turns to spit out his own insult, Bianca pops up beside them.

"I think you look great," Bianca says.

Charlie slides closer to her. "And you look pretty good yourself."

God, he's such a flirt.

The Evil Joes roll their eyes and walk up the driveway to Bailey's house. I give them a few moments to get ahead of me before I follow them.

"Thanks, Charlie," I say as I step away from my car. Bianca and Charlie are still lost in their conversation, but when I get halfway to the door, Charlie yells, "Hold up! Switch back with me!" He's running toward me, my phone in his outstretched hand. "She's texting again!"

"Oh yeah, yours is in my cupholder. My car is unlocked." I take the phone back and yep, there's a notification from Mom.

MOM: Take some pics! Have fun!

I give her a thumbs-up emoji and head inside, smiling at the fact that Bianca is still lingering next to my car, talking to Charlie.

I've spent countless hours at Bailey's house, but I almost don't recognize it when I step inside. Bailey's mom has blow-up mattresses scattered throughout her den, each piled high with pillows and blankets as if we've had a humongous sleepover. Nonna could get some ideas from this for the nights she expects us all to sleep at her house even though my house (and my bed!) is only two blocks away.

"Olivia!" Bailey's mom squeals when she sees me, then wraps me in a tight hug. She turns me toward the kitchen and says, "There are pancakes and fruit and muffins on the island. The coffee and juice bar are on the kitchen table. Help yourself!"

I make a plate and join Bailey and Mia on one of the mattresses.

"The dress code for every party should be pajamas," I say when I snuggle into my temporary bed.

"For real," Mia says. "And pancakes should be served at every meal."

"How'd the thing go at your grandmother's yesterday? I still haven't finished my questionnaire," Bailey says. "I'm about to put *Undecided* on everything and turn it in."

I let out a groan. "Yeah, same. I didn't finish mine either."

They both look at me, confused. "How'd you get away with that?" They know Nonna pretty well.

Here's my moment to tell them what's going on. I stumble around in my mind on what to say. How to explain it without feeling embarrassed. Even though the room is full of people, we're essentially in our own little bubble and I don't think Bailey and Mia are so friendly with the Evil Joes that they would spill this. I open my mouth to say the words, but Bailey speaks first.

"You know they'll probably show your entire questionnaire on the screen while you're giving your speech instead of just one or two answers from ours while we cross the stage to get our diploma. You're going to have to answer yours like you mean it!"

"It's so cool you get to give the opening speech!" Mia says, clapping her hands together. "I called it on the first day of freshman year. I knew you'd finish first or second. I wouldn't have gotten through half my classes without you."

Bianca finally shows up and drops down on the edge of the mattress. "Where have you been?" Mia asks.

"What? I was getting coffee," she answers.

And the explanation about off-campus PE and Coach Cantu dies in my throat. Why bring it up when it will be fixed tomorrow? There's really no reason why anyone else needs to know. This is a blip! Nothing to see here!

Mia's dad comes by with a trash bag a bit later to take our empty plates and cups while Bailey's mom gets everyone's attention from the front of the room. "Okay, girls! I thought it would be fun to take something off to college with you to remind you of these last four years!" She calls our names and then hands us each a white pillowcase monogrammed with our first name along the edge. "There's a jar of fabric pens next to each mattress. Pass your pillowcase around the room and write each other a quick note!"

The four of us pass ours between one another and I write a short note on each one with a purple marker. Bailey is headed to LSU, same as me, but Mia and Bianca are going out of state. I make sure they know how much I'll miss them. We then hand ours over to the mattress next to us in exchange for theirs. Pillowcases circle the room, and I'm only stumped when I get the Evil Joes'. I eyeball them from three mattresses away and wonder if they've gotten mine yet.

"Would it be too obvious if I draw skulls and crossbones on theirs?" I ask.

Mia laughs and Bailey says, "I thought y'all would be better by now."

"They're nice to you because you pass them the ball during games," I counter.

"Probably so," she admits.

I lean forward. "They put all my bras and underwear in a garbage bag and stuffed it in the back of Aunt Patrice's Suburban just before Aunt Patrice and Uncle Ronnie left Nonna's on the way to Florida for a week freshman year."

"Oh my God!" Bianca barks out.

"And while I'm pondering where my undies went, Aunt Patrice has laid them all out on the kitchen table of her Florida rental and sent a picture of them in the group text to ask whose they are."

"Okay, skulls and crossbones are appropriate," Bailey says.

I end up writing *I hope your dreams are as sweet as you!* on both and sign it with the letter O.

My phone dings and I see a text from Sophie.

SOPHIE: Did he sign it?

ME: Ugh no course is closed today

But it gets me thinking again about my dilemma. "Do any of you know anyone on the golf team?" I ask. I texted people from my class, but we are all beginners. It just occurred to me that people on the team probably have Coach Cantu's number.

Bailey looks up from the pillowcase she's writing on. "We have a golf team?" she asks.

I give her a head-tilt kind of nod and she's legitimately shocked to learn this.

"I don't," Mia says, but Bianca looks like she's really considering my question.

"I do. We had to take their team photo for yearbook. Let me think. . . . There's Lily Rodriquez, David Pham, Tanika Rogers, Chloe Kim, Chris Locke . . ."

Mia asks, "Locke still lives here? Didn't he move in middle school?"

Bianca shakes her head. "He was homeschooled in middle school so he could spend the day at the golf course. He's really good. But he came back to regular school sophomore year. I had English with him."

We had a few Chrises in our class when we were young, so we started calling him "Locke" as a way to differentiate between him and the others.

"He's in my calculus class this year," I add. "But I didn't know he played on the team."

"Why are you asking about golf?" Mia asks.

"I'm trying to get in touch with the golf coach."

They're satisfied with my answer and I have a list of people to reach out to as soon as this party is over. It feels good to have a plan. Bailey's mom calls for us to get together for some pictures on the mattresses in the middle of the room. It takes a while for everyone to reclaim their pillowcase, and the first thing I search for on mine is what the Evil Joes wrote.

Hope you don't mess up on your speech!
The whole family will be there xoxo JL MJ

God, they're the worst.

Once the party ends, I'm back in my car outside of Bailey's house, opening up my contacts list so I can call someone on the team for Coach Cantu's number. Out of all of the people Bianca listed on the golf team, Chris Locke's number is the only one I don't already have. And he's the last one I would call, anyway. He was so rude to me in Calculus. It's not my fault he can't tell an antiderivative from a derivative. I decide to call Tanika, since I know her the best.

Luckily, she answers on the third ring.

"Olivia, what's up?" she asks.

"Hey! I need your help. I'm trying to get in touch with Coach Cantu. Do you happen to have his number?"

I can tell she switches the call to speaker when she says, "Sending it to you now, but he won't answer. I'd be surprised if he has his phone on him at all. He's impossible to get in touch with." The frustration in her voice is obvious.

"Oh my God, how can one person be so friggin' hard to get in touch with? I should not be having this problem with today's technology! My mom is currently hours away from here and yet she still knows I'm sitting in my car in front of Bailey's house right this minute." Okay, I didn't mean to word-vomit all of that on her.

But for real—he may not have his phone on him?!

"I know. He's so old-school. If you don't get him, a few of us are meeting him for lunch at Silver Star. There's a tournament this week and even though it isn't a team event, we're still getting together to discuss the course and strategy since most of us haven't ever played there. We'll be there at noon."

There is an ounce of hope that I can handle this today and quit worrying about it. Checking the time on the dash, I see I've got thirty minutes until they're at the restaurant. "Thank you! Thank you! You have no idea how much this means to me!"

"Okay, okay, I got it. Good luck," she says, and ends the call.

I save Coach Cantu's contact, then pull up a message to him. After taking a deep breath, I type:

ME: Hi Coach Cantu! This is Olivia Perkins! I've been trying to reach you!

Whoa, way too many exclamation points. Delete, delete, delete.

ME: Coach Cantu, it's Olivia Perkins. I am in dire need of speaking to you. It is of the utmost importance

No, no. Too formal. Sounds so forced. God, why is this so hard?

ME: Hey Coach Cantu. This is Olivia Perkins and I really need to talk to you about my off campus PE form. I need to get one signed before they will let me graduate. Could you please text or call me back at your earliest convenience? Thank you so much!

I hit SEND before I can overthink it any more. And then stare at the screen until it shows that the message was delivered. At least I know where he'll be in half an hour. I race home so I can change out of these pajamas and be ready to hunt him down if he doesn't call or text me back by then.

I'm in and out of my house in ten minutes, throwing on a cuter version of the athletic shorts and a tee I was wearing earlier, and then I'm back in the car, headed to Silver Star.

It's 11:55 by the time I pull into the parking lot of the restaurant. Watching every car that pulls in, I finally see Coach

Cantu get out of his truck, and I leap out of my car, chasing after him.

"Coach!" I scream through the parking lot. I'm going faster than I think, and when he stops to turn around, I dang near run him over.

"Olivia! What are you doing here?" he asks.

I have the blank form in my hand and I'm shoving it at him. Then I'm digging in my pocket for a pen. "You forgot to sign my form for my off-campus PE. They're saying I can't graduate without it."

He takes the form and the pen from me, looks at it for a few seconds, then back at me. He frowns and I'm hoping it's because he's realizing his mistake and nothing else.

"Let's walk inside so we can talk a moment," he says. I follow him into the restaurant and notice the group of students off to the side. Tanika gives me a small wave. I wave back but can't force a smile on my lips until I know all of this is going to be okay.

Coach steers me toward a seating area just inside the foyer. He sets the paper and pen on the table near the chair and pulls out a notebook from his back pocket.

It's small and worn and he has to flip a bunch of pages before he gets to what he's looking for, but by his nod and grimace, I can tell when he's finally found it. And it doesn't seem like it's good news for me.

Coach Cantu turns the notebook around so I can read

what's on the page. My name is at the top followed by a bunch of dates, times, and numbers.

"You didn't meet the requirements, Olivia. The dates show when we met as a class. You got credit for the time you were there. Since most days you were significantly late and there were quite a few days where you never showed up at all, you only got credit for the minutes you were there. And those missed minutes added up. I'm sorry."

I am stunned.

It takes a few seconds before words actually form in my brain. "You docked me for being late?" I finally spit out.

"Did you read the packet I gave you on the first day?" he asks. The thing about Coach Cantu is he's a really nice guy. Soft-spoken and patient, he's easily one of the nicest teachers I've ever had. But this right here is throwing me. Is he really not going to sign this form because I was late a few times?

He's looking at me and I realize I haven't answered his question.

"I thought I did," I answer. Honestly, I didn't think too much about this class, since it seemed like a breeze compared to the rest of my course load.

"I gave everyone three excused tardies and two excused absences, no questions asked. Once you ran out of those, the tardies and the absences started counting against you. Halfway through the semester I offered several opportunities to make up time by helping with local matches. You didn't take me up on any of those. When I was recording all the hours for the school, I realized just how behind you were and was going to let you know. There was a clinic you could have helped with, but you didn't show up to class that day. You left me no choice."

I don't even remember skipping the last day. At all. I've had a ton of work finishing up my AP classes and getting ready for exams. My mind is racing. Spinning. I can't not graduate because of golf! I don't even like golf!

"I have to graduate. I'm salutatorian."

His face lights up. "Oh, that's wonderful! How exciting!"

I'm shaking my head. "It's not wonderful if this class ruins all of that."

He bends his head a little closer to me. "If you worked so hard on your other classes to achieve such high honors, why didn't you give the same attention to mine?"

What am I going to say to that? Tell him I thought his class was a joke and didn't mean anything?

I shrug instead and give him the most pitiful face I can manage.

Coach Cantu picks up the paper again and studies it, then glances back at his notebook. "When is this form due?"

"A week from today."

He nods. "I'll make you a deal. You owe me a lot of time and I could use your help during the tournament that starts tomorrow. Four full days. You give me that and I'll apply it to the class time you missed and call it even."

"Yes! Yes, of course. Whatever I have to do."

"Okay, wonderful!" He's genuinely happy to help me. And now I feel bad for blowing this class off all semester. "Plan to be at Ellerbe Hills all day Tuesday through Friday. We start early. Seven thirty in the morning!"

And then it dawns on me. If I work this tournament, I will be there when I'm supposed to be at graduation parties with my friends. I feel my throat getting tight and my eyes starting to water, but I reel it in and swallow it down. A bunch of parties won't matter if I can't graduate with my class.

"Lily," Coach Cantu calls out, then motions for her to join us. I spare another glance at the group of players waiting near the host stand, and by the way they're all huddled together, I can tell they're speculating about why I'm here.

"Hey, Coach, hey, Olivia," Lily says when she joins us.

"Hey," I squeak out.

Coach gestures to me. "Olivia will be helping out at the tournament, too. Will you get her added to the security list as my assistant? She'll also need a name badge."

"Will she need a shirt, too?" Lily asks.

"Yes. And a visor." He turns to me. "Just wear some khaki shorts and whatever top you want in the morning. Lily will give you a shirt you can change into when you get there."

"Will I need to bring anything else?" I ask.

"Sunblock," Lily says. "Your driver's license to get your badge in the morning, and money for lunch and drinks unless you're a member of the club."

I feel like I need to be taking notes or something.

The host approaches Coach to ask him a question and he steps away to answer her.

"Do you mind me asking why you're coming on as Coach's assistant at the last minute?"

I can tell she's really curious why I'm here, so I give her the most basic answer I can. "Just making up a few hours from his PE class." I don't mention my graduating hinges on it. "I'm stuck helping with the tournament."

And then I cringe at my own words. "I don't mean it like that. It's awesome y'all are here. Competing. It's just I have no idea what I'm doing. I know absolutely nothing about golf."

Her head tilts. "But you took a semester of it?"

"Yeah. I guess you could say I didn't pay that much attention." I hold my hands out wide. "Which is why I'm here."

"Well, you'll get a crash course. This tournament is golf on steroids. Everyone wants to place high, and there are still some spots left on college teams, so it gets pretty cutthroat. For a lot of players, this is their last chance."

"Will you play in it?"

A frown appears on her face for just a second before it's gone. "No. I'm not ranked high enough, so I offered to help Coach. Getting hired by Ellerbe Hills Country Club is great for him, but this tournament is a huge deal and he needs all the help he can get."

I nod toward the group waiting not far away. "But the rest of the team is playing?"

Lily glances back at the group. "About half. Out of the girls, Chloe and Em Beth are seniors like me and hoping to get spots for next year, so they're playing. Tanika is playing, but she's a junior. She'll get an offer before she starts senior year. She's that good."

"Oh wow," I say.

Coach walks back over and says, "They're ready for us." Then he turns to me. "Do you want to stay for lunch? Get to know the team?"

"Oh!" I say, surprised by the invitation. I look down at the Nike shorts and tee I'm wearing. I'm in no way dressed to eat here. "I'd love to, but I need to get a few things in order if I'm planning to spend the rest of the week working."

His face breaks out in a big smile. "We'll see you first thing in the morning!"

And then he hustles the team to the waiting table while I'm still standing there trying to figure out what just happened.

"Joining the team?" a voice behind me asks.

I whip around and see Chris Locke. Ugh.

"Uh, no. But I'll be helping out."

"Really? Helping out how?" He's probably worried I'm going to screw up his game or something.

I stand up a little straighter and say, "Not sure, but whatever Coach needs."

"Just don't get in the way. You won't be the teacher's pet out on the course," he says, then moves past me to join his group at the table in the other room, not even bothering to say bye.

I sink down into the nearest chair. How could this one class have turned into such a disaster?

I'll have to call Mom and tell her what's going on. There's no way I can miss all those parties without her knowing. And she'll for sure know when my phone is at the Ellerbe Hills all day for four days in a row.

But I absolutely hate telling her this. Hate that she'll know how close I came to almost screwing everything up. Jake is the screwup in our immediate family, not me. I mean, I love him, but it's the truth! Jake is the one who will take five to six years to get his degree—if he finishes!—not me. He's the one who breaks his leg because someone dares him he can't climb up the side of his fraternity house. I'm the easy one. The good one. The one who has it all figured out. The one most like Mom.

I know what Mom will say:

I told you not to do an off-campus class.

You took on too much this semester.

I knew this was too much.

We're on our way home.

It's that last one that really gets me. It took forever to get her to agree to let me stay home alone while she and my dad were gone. If I tell her what happened, she'll be on the road back immediately because this will be all the proof she needs that I'm not responsible enough to take care of myself. As if her being home would change this situation at all.

I will never hear the end of this. Ever. I mean, it's not like I can get Sophie and Charlie and Wes to cover for me. There's no way I could be at the country club all week while they man my phone and be me.

It would be dumb to try to do that.

Dumb.

My thumb hovers above Mom's number in my contact list, and I can feel heat rising up my chest. Suddenly I stand back up.

I'm about to be dumb and pray that Charlie, Sophie, and Wes will be dumb with me.

8 P.M.

Truth #3: There's nothing worse
than peeing in the woods

Monday, May 9th, Afternoon

Olivia

I head straight to Nonna's and find the three people I'm looking for
sitting at her kitchen table. Nonna and Papa's shop, Greenhouse
Flowers and Gifts, is closed on Mondays (except during the
holidays), so it's not unusual to find a crowd here for lunch.

"What's up?" I say when I come through the back door.

A chorus of *Hey*s bounces through the room. Papa is
also here, along with Charlie's little sister, Sara, and his parents, Uncle Charles and Aunt Ayin, who must also be off
work today. Charlie's parents met when they both worked for
Doctors Without Borders in the Philippines, where Charlie's
mom is originally from. Now they work for a local hospital, but
I can never keep up with their crazy schedule.

There are three large pizzas spread out along the counter with breadsticks and cheese sauce. It's rare that Nonna doesn't cook, even if it's only lunch. "Pizza?" I go straight for a paper plate before I even hear why there's takeout. "Oh, Sweep the Kitchen. My favorite."

"Mom had a meeting at church about the reception for the bishop," Uncle Charles says.

The new bishop is about the only thing that would get her out of the house during mealtime.

"I had to threaten them within an inch of their life to make sure they left you a piece or two," Sophie says.

"You were supposed to be here an hour ago," Charlie adds. "We can't be blamed if you're late."

Wes pushes the box of breadsticks to me. He waits until I'm at the table next to him and leans close to whisper, "Did you get it all worked out?"

I let out a nervous laugh. "Funny you should ask. It's a little more complicated than I thought it would be."

Our eyes dart around the room, none of us wanting to bring it up in front of the others. We make a silent agreement to talk about it once we're back at my house.

The back door opens and Aunt Maggie Mae and the Evil Joes walk inside. Looks like Leo must have gone back home since he's not with them.

"Mom isn't here?" Aunt Maggie Mae asks. The pizza is a dead giveaway.

All three of them have the same pouty face once Uncle Charles gives the explanation.

"Well, shoot. The girls wanted to look at some of her old hats. They're invited to a Derby Day luncheon!" Aunt Maggie Mae turns to face us. "Olivia, did you get an invite to that one?"

"Is that Justina's party?" I ask. I heard talk of it this morning at Bailey's.

"It sure is," she answers.

"I sure didn't," I say. Justina and I hardly ever overlap, so it would have been more awkward if I had been invited to her party.

They all try to look sad for me, but it doesn't really reach the eyes. "Well, that's too bad. It'll be the highlight of the week," Aunt Maggie Mae says, then looks at Sophie. "Do your friends at your school not have parties thrown for them?" Her condescending tone spears Sophie right between the eyes.

Sophie shrugs. "Not like y'all do here. We have a big party for everyone on Thursday night, but that's about it."

Right as Aunt Maggie Mae is about to open her mouth again, I say, "But I know I got invited to something with a hat. Mom bought one for me a week ago. I think it's a tea party or something?"

Now it's Aunt Maggie Mae's turn to ponder what I got invited to that the Evil Joes didn't, because I happen to know Sarah Brooks dislikes the Evil Joes almost as much as I do.

Luckily, Papa steps in before it can get ugly. "Girls, y'all can go on up and look to see what Nonna has. I think all her old hats are in boxes in the hall closet."

The three of them leave the room and Charlie signals that we should wrap it up here and head to my house. Sophie and Wes clear the table and put the dishes in the dishwasher while Charlie and I put away the uneaten pizza.

"I'll take these out to the recycling bin," I say, wrestling with the large empty cardboard boxes. I step out of the back door and almost trip over someone sitting on the back steps. I catch myself but not the boxes as they scatter everywhere.

"Oh! Sorry!" Leo says, one hand steadying me and the other reaching for the closest pizza box on the ground.

We both stumble around until I'm holding half of the boxes and he's holding the other half.

"We're making a habit of meeting like this," I say as we both head to the recycling bin.

"Didn't realize what we were doing here until we were in the car on the way over. I don't think they need my help looking at hats."

"They could use more help than you think," I say, hearing the insult in my words and cringing just a little. I have to remember he actually likes them. "You could have come in and had some pizza," I add.

He gives me a look like he's questioning whether or not I truly believe the words coming out of my mouth. "With you and Charlie and Sophie and Wes? Would you have invited me to sit down at your table?"

We're side by side, arms full, so I knock my shoulder into him playfully. "I would have thrown you a piece of pizza from across the room at the very least."

He laughs and knocks me back. "Then I'm regretting staying out on the porch for sure."

It's not easy bending and folding the boxes so they'll fit inside the container. Leo ends up putting the folded boxes on the ground and stomping to flatten them.

"That should do it," he says as he stuffs the last one in.

"Now I feel like I should throw you two pieces for being such a good helper!"

"And maybe I should fold you up and put you in the recycling!"

We're both chuckling as we head back toward the house.

"You ready?" Charlie asks from the open door.

"Yeah. I'm ready," I say to Charlie, then turn to Leo. "See you later."

"I'll be on the porch anytime you need me," he says.

I catch up with Charlie, Wes, and Sophie as they are walking down the driveway.

"What was that about?" Wes asks.

I shrug. "Nothing. He helped me throw away the boxes."

I speed-walk ahead of him so he'll quit looking at me like I'm a traitor.

As soon as I unlock the door to my house, Sophie drops into one of the chairs at the kitchen table. "Okay, back to business. Did that coach sign your form?"

"No," I answer.

Sophie stands up quickly, almost knocking her chair over.

"Whoa, tiger. Where ya going?" Wes asks.

She drops back into her chair for the second time. "I . . . just . . . How could he not sign it?"

I tilt my head to the side. "Well, it's mostly my fault." And then I tell them everything.

Charlie leans back in his chair. "No biggie, then. You go hang out at the golf course, get a little sun, nothing to it."

"Why are you making that face?" Wes asks me. He turns to Sophie. "It's not good when she makes that face."

"There's a hitch," I say.

Charlie is shaking his head.

I nod right back to him.

"What hitch?" Sophie asks.

"I'm not telling Mom and Dad what happened. I'll never live it down. And the whole family will find out and I'd rather poke my eye out than listen to what Aunt Maggie Mae will say about it."

"Okay," Wes says, drawing out the word. "Still not getting the hitch."

I point to the line of invitations hanging from the twine. "I'm supposed to be at a luncheon every day this week. And

Mom is watching my every move. She'll know I'm not there, and she'll also know I'm at Ellerbe Hills Country Club all day instead. There will be no hiding it from her."

"I know where this is going," Charlie says. "I had your phone for ninety minutes and Aunt Lisa texted seventeen times. Seven. Teen."

I hold my hands out as if I can stop them from bailing before I even ask them to help. "We can switch up. If y'all are willing, I know we can pull this off. And I'll owe you forever."

Sophie reaches out and squeezes my hand. "I wouldn't have gotten through Christmas break without you, so you know I'm in." Then she nudges Wes in the side hard enough to make him grunt.

"Oof. I'm in, too," he says. Sophie leans over and plants a loud kiss on his cheek.

"We can work together," she whispers to him.

"Am I the only one who realizes how completely insane this is?" Charlie asks, then drops his head on the table. "I guess I'm in, too," he mumbles.

I jump up from the table and give each of them a big hug.

"I can't help on Wednesday, though," Sophie says. "Mom and I are shopping for a graduation dress."

Charlie says, "I can do Wednesday. But I can't do Thursday. Working for Nonna all day at the shop."

"I can do Thursday," Wes volunteers.

And I could cry.

"Okay, so I'll do tomorrow," Sophie says. "Then Charlie has Wednesday and Wes has Thursday. What about Friday?"

"We'll figure it out later if we haven't been busted by then. I'll be shocked if all three of us are texting your mom and she doesn't figure out it's not you," Wes says.

Sophie moves to the line of invitations. "What's the party tomorrow?"

"There are actually two," I say. "A luncheon for Sarah Brooks. I think the theme is tea party? It's the one with the hat. And tomorrow night is a toga party."

Wes's head pops up. "I think I was invited to that." Then he turns to Sophie. "There's a toga party tomorrow night. You're coming, too."

She laughs and lightly punches him in the arm. "Thanks for the advance notice."

Charlie nods. "Yeah, I got an invite, too." He turns to look at me. "But you should be finished by then, right? So we can all go?"

"Yes, I'm sure I'll be done by the afternoon. And, Sophie, hopefully I can get away for an hour so I can make an appearance at the luncheon. I really would hate to miss it."

"Okay, good!" Sophie says. "Now to find some sheets for the toga party. . . ."

Once every closet and cabinet of my house is raided, we're back downstairs, sitting in the den, trying to find something on TV.

"We should think about dinner soon," Charlie says.

Wes and Sophie are lying on the couch. "You know Nonna has something fixed," Wes says.

Just as Charlie is about to say something else, he, Wes, and I all get a text at the same time.

"Okay, so I'm feeling a little left out," Sophie says when we reach for our phones.

Charlie jumps up from his chair and pumps his fist in the air. "Hell yes!"

I swipe open the message and it's a picture of a wagon wheel with a message below that reads 8 *P.M.* "Tonight? It's Monday!" I say.

Wes is showing Sophie the text. "What is this, like some sort of Bat-Signal?" she asks.

"Exactly! Party tonight!" Charlie yells.

"We're all right here," I say.

The Wagon Wheel is an old bar just outside of town. It went out of business like twenty years ago and the land it sits on was bought by a family with sons at our school—Miller and Will Hudson. They love throwing parties there because it's less likely to get busted, but they give almost no warning. It's their way of keeping things from getting out of hand, since there's less time for word to spread.

"I have to be at the course at seven thirty in the morning, so we can't stay too late," I say. I wouldn't miss this for anything, but I am a little worried about how a late night tonight could make tomorrow even worse than it'll already be.

Charlie looks at me like I've lost it. "It's Senior Party Week. We're not coming home early!"

Yeah, tomorrow is going to be exactly as bad as I think.

We arrive at the Wagon Wheel at eight o'clock on the dot. The building itself is a square cinder-block structure with a rusty metal roof. There's no sign, just a very large wooden wheel that looks a hundred years old leaning against the side of the building. The parking lot is more grass than gravel and there's actually a thin tree poking out of a side window. Inside, the long bar is still in place, but dirt took over the floor years ago. There are a few holes in the roof that make it cold in the winter, but for the most part, it's a pretty cool place to have a party when you're in high school and have nowhere else to go.

And just because we got here right on time does not mean we're early. There are probably twenty cars already parked in the field next to the building.

Everyone lives for these parties.

"I can't believe I've never been here," Sophie says.

Wes shrugs. "Well, the few times since Christmas they've had a party, we were in Minden hanging out there."

Inside, the music is loud and the only light comes from the zigzag of twinkle lights hanging from the ceiling.

There's a keg in the center of the room and people are lined up, red cups in hand.

"I'm glad you drove, Wes!" Charlie says as he gets in line. A few minutes later, he's back with a cup for Sophie, me, and himself, and a bottle of water for Wes.

The place gets packed quickly, and I decide to limit myself to one beer because the bathroom options here are not good. It's basically *head outside and find a hidden spot in the woods.*

No thank you.

Charlie heads out to the area that was once a dance floor but Wes, Sophie, and I hang back. My phone vibrates in my back pocket, so I pull it out and see there's a text from Mom:

MOM: Where in the world are you?

ME: A party on some land some friends own

MOM: Who's driving?

ME: Wes. And he's drinking water

MOM: Okay. Text me when you leave

I'm shoving my phone back in my pocket when I hear someone beside me say, "Coach wouldn't tell me why you're suddenly interested in golf."

Spinning around, I see Locke standing there and I have to stop myself from rolling my eyes.

At least Coach Cantu isn't putting it out there as to how bad I screwed up. "I took his class. Why would I do that if I wasn't interested in golf?"

"I've never seen you at a tournament, but the last week of senior year, you'll be there every day?"

My lip curls. "Why are you worried about what I'm doing?"

"It's just surprising. You're the last one I would have picked to give up all those parties to hang out at the golf course."

Yep. He's got me there. So I decide to ignore him and turn my attention back to the dance floor. Charlie has noticed I'm talking to Locke and I know I'm going to get interrogated later.

"I'm surprised you're here," I say to Locke, still not looking at him. "Don't you have to be there pretty early tomorrow?"

He holds up a water bottle, right in my line of sight. "This may be the last Wagon Wheel party. Couldn't miss it."

I hold up my red Solo cup. "Yeah, same!"

Miller and Will are on a makeshift stage on the other side of the dance floor, where they're DJ-ing with a laptop and one of the biggest speakers I've ever seen. Will holds a big flashlight and Miller has a microphone. As they randomly point the spotlight on someone and call out their name, that person has to show their moves.

It's not long before that light finds Charlie.

"Charlie Messina!" Miller yells. And now Charlie is doing some dance move I have never seen and definitely never want to again. But of course, because it's Charlie, there are cheers from everyone in the room before Miller and Will move on to the next victim.

Wes steps in front of Sophie and me. "Come on, it's time to dance," he says, pulling us toward Charlie. And since Locke didn't bother saying bye to me earlier, I follow without another word.

It gets hot quick with so many bodies packed into this building and no air moving at all except for what's flowing in through the open back doors.

I fan myself with my hands and lean close enough to Sophie so she can hear me above the music. "I'm getting some water!"

She nods as I walk away. I have to dig in two ice chests before I find a bottle.

"Is there another one in there?"

I look up and see Leo.

"Oh, hey!" I say, then reach back into the ice chest, pulling a second bottle out for him.

"Thanks," he says, when I hand it over.

He's a little sweaty, too, and those curls have kicked into high gear. I look around for the Evil Joes but don't see them.

"They're outside," he says, motioning to the open back doors.

"I guess I'm that easy to read," I say.

He gives me a lopsided grin. "None of y'all look at me

without also checking to see where they are. It's kind of funny."

"Always good to know where your enemies are," I say with a laugh, except we both know I'm not joking.

"Nonna set anyone up on any more dates lately?" he asks, changing the subject. "The girls were telling me about that. Sounded hilarious."

This stops me short. "Did *the girls* happen to tell you about the date they set Soph up on?"

"Movie date, right? What's wrong with that?"

My mouth is open like a fish out of water. "Oh, it was a movie, all right. Is that all they said?"

He can tell from my tone this is not going the way he thought it would. He holds his hands up and says, "Calm down, I'm not trying to make you mad."

Calm down. Those two words are like waving red in front of a bull.

"Oh, I'm calm. You need to get the facts straight. Ask *the girls*."

I walk off and join Wes and Sophie back on the dance floor. As much as I try, though, it's hard not to keep track of where Leo is. He's moved across the room to a beer pong game with a group that includes the Evil Joes and their boyfriends. And it's bad that I watch him long enough to notice that when he misses, someone on his team takes his drink for him. I guess he's their designated driver tonight.

Needing some distance so I don't completely embarrass myself, I track down Mia and Bailey on the other side of the room.

"Yay! There's Olivia!" Bailey squeals when I join them.

They're sitting on top of the bar. Mia holds out her hand. "Hop up here. It's a perfect view of the room."

I take her hand and she pulls me up. I squeeze in between them. We people-watch, and even though I was trying to get away from staring at Leo, I find this is the perfect location to do exactly that.

Bailey leans close so I can hear her over the music. "There's a bunch of us staying at my house tonight if you want to come over."

I turn toward her. "Aw, I can't. Sophie is in town and staying at my house." I don't mention how early I have to get up in the morning.

"We figured but wanted to ask anyway."

I try not to cringe. This happens a lot and I feel a little awkward that I'm always turning down Bailey's invitation. Thankfully, Miller and Will put a new victim in their spotlight, so the tension passes on the rejected invite.

After a few songs, Sophie weaves through the crowd to find me. She says hi to Bailey and Mia and they return her greeting, but that's it. Soph leans against the bar next to me. "As much as I was trying to avoid it, I've got to go to the bathroom. And since the bathroom is actually a bush in the woods, I can't go alone."

And as soon as she says the words, I feel the same way.

"Yeah, I need to go, too." I scoot off the bar, then turn to Bailey and Mia. "Y'all need to go?"

They both decline, and Sophie drags me out of the back of the building and doesn't stop until we're surrounded by trees and bushes. Just one of the indignities of partying in an abandoned building.

Sophie pulls a few napkins out of her pocket. "Here," she says, handing me one. For her first time here, she's more prepared than I am. "We have field parties all the time. You always need a napkin or two on you."

We both stand there a minute with our hands on the waistbands of our shorts. Even though we can still hear the music, we can also hear the birds in the trees and the unknown creatures rustling in the underbrush. It's really dark out here, and scenes from every horror movie I've ever seen run through my head.

"I'm always scared something is going to bite my butt," I admit.

Sophie laughs at me but then stomps around in the area around us, making really loud growling noises.

"That probably bought us a few feet of unoccupied space," she says, once she's finished.

"Well, we better not waste it!"

Once we're done, we start navigating our way back to the building. We're almost out of the woods when Sophie grabs my arm and pulls me back.

"Look who it is," she whispers.

About twenty feet away, the Evil Joes are looking for their own bathroom spot. We tiptoe back into the woods, keeping them in sight. They almost glow in the dark in the white shirts they're wearing, making it easy to keep up with them. We wait until they've settled in, then Sophie throws this big stick she found on the ground next to us, chucking it just to the left of where they're squatting. They both scream bloody murder and Sophie and I almost fall over trying to hold our laughter in.

The Joes sprint back to the Wagon Wheel, pulling up their jeans as they run, and it's a good thing I've already used the bathroom or I'd pee all over myself.

"Okay, I feel like we're finally even for the drive-in movie," Sophie says.

It took forever to drag Charlie off the dance floor. He would have been the last person there if we let him.

"You sure were dancing with Bianca a lot tonight," I say.

Charlie and I are in the backseat and Sophie is riding

shotgun. He turns to me. "Did I see you talking to Locke?"

"I talked to him for like two minutes. You danced with Bianca for like two hours." I hold my hands up. "Don't get me wrong, I love her! Y'all would be cute together."

I'm teasing him because Charlie has sworn off girlfriends. He wants to start college single so he is free to mingle. His words, not mine.

"She's fun. That's it," he says. "And she's going somewhere far. Like Georgia. Or Alabama."

"That's not that far," Wes says.

"Far enough. And what are you saying? You can't wait until you and Sophie are in the same town and she's only thirty minutes away right now."

Wes grins into the rearview mirror. "Yeah, you got me."

Before long, we're pulling up in front of my house. Sophie is staying the night so she's here to man the phone, since I have to be at the golf course so early.

I let myself inside, shower, and get ready for bed while she and Wes do their good-byes. Climbing under the covers, I'm nervous about tomorrow all of a sudden. I grab my phone from the bedside table and start googling *golf*. And *golf tournaments*. And watch videos and study every picture I come across.

Golf is a big deal.

It's clear I didn't pay much attention to it this entire semester, because most of the common terms seem foreign to me. It's probably the only sport where you want the lowest score. And I feel like that shouldn't be new news! Though in my defense, most of our classes were spent hitting balls at the range or on the putting green working on our technique.

But these tournaments are the big leagues. And I get why. A good game can make the difference between having a spot on a college team (and a full ride) or not.

Finally Sophie comes in, and it's not long before she's crawling into the other side of my bed. I put my phone away and try to get some sleep.

Tomorrow is going to be a long day.

Southern Tea Party
IN HONOR OF
Sarah Brooks

Fairfield Bed & Breakfast
Tuesday, May 10th, Noon
Hats are encouraged

Truth #4: Golf-ball pyramids are overrated

Tuesday, May 10th, Morning

Olivia

Six a.m. comes early. When my phone's alarm goes off, there is a rumble of moans and groans from the other side of the bed.

"Turn it off," Sophie says. "Make it stop." Just enough light filters into the room for me to see Sophie burrow down in the bed and drag a pillow over her head.

"Sorry," I whisper, and tiptoe to the bathroom. Thankfully, I had my shower last night so this morning is just throwing my hair up and brushing my teeth. I pull on the pair of shorts I found in Mom's dresser and a tee with my school logo. From the pics I saw last night, it looks like all the girls wear tennis skirts, but Coach said to come in khaki shorts, so yay for team spirit. Even though they aren't there as a school team. Whatever.

"Sophie," I whisper. "I'm about to go, but I need to switch phones with you."

She makes a grunting sound. Then says, "It's charging on the desk. Leave yours there."

Phone swap complete, I make a cup of coffee to go and grab a granola bar for the ride to Ellerbe Hills.

I spend the drive imagining what my job will be. Maybe I'll keep the scores for players? Or I'll be taking pics and posting them to their social media? That would be cool.

Not going to lie, I'm a little smug when I pull back up to the guard station. It's the same guy who wouldn't let me through yesterday.

He steps up to my window and gives me that same look. "Can I help you?"

"Yes! I'm meeting Coach Cantu here. I'm his assistant."

"Name?"

"Olivia Perkins."

He runs his finger down the page and stops when he gets to my name.

"ID?"

Really? Who else would try to sneak in here to work?

I hand over my ID and he holds it up to a small camera on the wall of the guard station.

"Olivia Perkins. Here with John Cantu."

He hands it back, then pushes a button just inside the small building and the gate across the driveway swings open.

I feel victorious.

The driveway winds through a wooded area, then opens onto the greenest grass I've ever seen. It's breathtaking, honestly. And then the clubhouse comes into view. *Majestic* is the best word I can come up with. The main building is two stories of red brick with wraparound porches and floor-to-ceiling windows. Crape myrtles and big ferns and rosebushes fill the flower beds, and there's a fountain front and center. All this to hit a small white ball into an equally small hole.

Coach Cantu is waiting for me on the sidewalk, holding a steaming cup of coffee.

I give him a small wave, but he looks down at his watch and I check Sophie's phone. It's 7:36.

"Sorry. Won't happen again," I say. Will he add these six minutes to the time I owe?

"Let's get moving. We need to get everything set up."

I follow him toward the clubhouse. "When do the players come?"

"Today is a practice day. Not every player will come out today, only the ones who want a full practice to mirror their first day's play tomorrow. They'll go through the course on the same schedule so there's nothing left to the imagination when it really counts. For the out-of-towners, it's important to run it all through at least once before the tournament begins. Especially a new course like this since most of these kids haven't ever played here before."

"So, you're not here as a coach, then? Will it be weird?"

"I'm here for the club. But my players know they can ask me anything," he says.

"Do you think there will be a lot of players practicing today?" I ask.

"If they want any chance of winning this thing, they'll show up."

Well, okay then.

Coach Cantu opens a door on the backside of the building, and I'm staring at huge metal bins full of golf balls, a tall stack of green trays, and a few pyramid-shape basket-looking things.

"Each spot at the range needs practice balls. Let me show you how it's done."

Coach grabs a regular bucket and fills it up with golf balls, setting it outside the door on a grassy area. Then he picks up one of the green square trays, putting it on the ground next to the bucket. He goes back inside the room once more and picks up the oddly pyramid-shape metal thingy. He sets it right on top of the green tray and it snaps into place. Then he pours balls from the bucket into the opening on top. Once it's full, he very gently lifts the metal part off the tray, leaving behind a perfectly shaped pyramid of golf balls.

"Whoa," I say. "That's cool."

Coach points toward the range. "There are twenty-five spots on the range for players to warm up. Each spot needs balls stacked exactly like this. Once a golfer finishes his warm-up, you'll stack a new pyramid of balls for the next player."

I'm nodding along as if these instructions make total sense. And then he's gone, walking toward the front of the giant clubhouse.

So I guess I'm not here to take pics for their social media.

It's logical to take the supplies to each spot before trying to make the pyramid because there's no way to move it without everything collapsing, but I didn't take into account how heavy a bucket of golf balls is. So now I'm sweating. Profusely. I get everything situated next to the first space, ready to lift the metal mold off. But then it snags on the side of the pyramid and balls scatter in every direction. I try to build it back up by hand but that's an even bigger disaster. So I start over. Three tries until I get my first perfect pyramid.

And then I look down the line. Twenty-four more spots to go.

By the time I've finished my fifth pyramid, Lily shows up. She hands me a collared short-sleeve shirt that matches the one Coach is wearing and a badge with my name on it.

"Thanks," I say.

"No problem. That badge will allow you into any area." She starts to turn away but then adds with a laugh, "You'll make all the parents jealous."

I laugh, too, even though I don't get the joke.

Lily gets busy marking names on little chalkboards of

players who have reserved a spot on the driving range while I continue to make ball pyramids. I will dream about this shape. Everything I look at morphs into it.

Players start arriving before I can finish, so now there's a line waiting for the few remaining spots.

There's a girl in a white tennis skirt and she's tapping—TAPPING—her foot at me. "We were told the practice range would be ready when we got here," she says.

I look up at her, sweat running down my face, and blow a loose chunk of hair out of my eye. She scrunches up her nose at me.

I want to put a hex on her pyramid.

Lily finally sees my predicament and we knock out the last three spots together.

Coach Cantu walks up just as we move out of the way and a player steps up into the space. "We can't have this happen tomorrow. It will throw everyone off."

"Yes, Coach," I mumble. "What should I do now?"

Coach motions to a small area near a bench. "Wait back here silently while they warm up. Once a player is done, refill the balls for that spot. If anyone needs anything . . . water, towel, tees, batteries . . . they will let you know. Inside the clubhouse is the pro shop. They can either give you money for what they need or they can charge it to their account if they have one. Most of the clubs in the state are in the same network, so they can charge it to their home club."

"Okay, I can do that."

He's about to walk away but stops and adds, "I gave my players from your school your number in case they need me but can't find me."

Oh, God. I'll have to tell Sophie so she can relay any messages to me. And I want to scream at him *Maybe carry a phone!*

I move away from the line of golfers so I'm not distracting but not too far. Looking down at the shirt Lily brought me, I really need to change but am afraid to leave my post, so I throw on the collared shirt over the tee I'm wearing, using it as a cover to wiggle out of the tee while trying to keep the shirt down and not expose myself to everyone. I must look completely ridiculous.

I ball my tee up and drop it next to my bag. I've only had the new shirt on for a few seconds but it's already getting a little sweaty.

God, this heat sucks.

Trying to take my mind off how miserable I am, I concentrate on the players. It doesn't take long to realize that not all of them hit the ball the same way. Some have a funny little ritual. The players from my school arrived a few minutes ago, so I pay particular attention to them. Along with Chloe, Tanika, and Em Beth, Lily told me Locke, David Pham, and Cal Rivers will play in this tournament as well.

Chloe uses her club to drag a ball off the little pyramid, careful not to let the whole structure fall apart. Knowing how easily they come tumbling down, I'm in awe of her. Then she lines herself up—but before she swings, she does this little hip wiggle. Then goes up on her tiptoes and back down, then wiggles again. Finally, she swings. She hits four balls with one club before changing it out for another one, but the routine is the exact same thing.

I scan down the line and watch the guys. They all seem to have a personalized routine, too. Cal holds his club above his head and does some sort of stretch before settling in for his swing. Every. Time.

It's fascinating.

Along with the different warm-up routines, it's clear that the part of the club where your hands go can come in lots of different colors, too. The ones we used for class were all white and pretty banged up after years of use and abuse, but Tanika's is hot pink and Locke's is a boring black (no surprise there).

And all the players seem to be totally in the zone. It's very quiet out here. No chitchat at all. Just that *thwack* sound when the club hits the ball. Just as Locke pulls his club back to swing, Sophie's phone blares in my back pocket. Locke stutters on his follow-through and ends up missing his ball but hitting the pyramid. Balls scatter everywhere.

I'm digging my phone out, trying to silence it as quickly as I can.

Locke says, "Turn your ringer off."

While David adds, "And keep it off."

Em Beth gives me a small smile. "It's okay, you didn't know."

I'm embarrassed. I've never been so spectacularly bad at anything in my life as I am at this.

Unlocking the phone to answer it, I don't even look at who's calling. But I'm not surprised when I hear Sophie's voice.

"Your mom is already texting. I thought it would be easy to answer her questions, but I'm overthinking it, I know."

I take a few steps away from the players so the sound of my voice doesn't completely ruin their whole day.

"What does she want?" I whisper.

"Why are you whispering?" she asks.

"Because I'm already at the golf course and this is some serious business, I'm discovering. I thought they were going to kill me when the phone rang."

"Oh no! Sorry! I should have texted."

"No, it's okay. What does she want?"

She lets out a breath. "She wanted to tell me good morning. And did I know my plans for the day. I was still asleep, so honestly, she caught me a little off guard. I know there's the luncheon at noon and the toga party tonight, but is there something else I'm supposed to be doing today?"

"Sorry, she's just like that. Wait, is your mom not?" My mom and Sophie's mom are twins and I've thought all this time that Sophie had to deal with the same stuff I did when it came to our moms.

"No. She'll probably text me once today just to check in, but all you need to say is *All good! Hanging with O!* and she'll be fine."

Okay, now that's not fair.

"Just text her that you're hanging loose until the luncheon. I'm going to try to get there right at noon. I'll make some excuse why I can't stay until the end, then haul it back here. After the luncheon, tell her we're all together working on our togas or something. Hopefully, I won't be here too long today."

"Okay, that works. The invitation says the party is at some bed-and-breakfast. I'll be out front a few minutes early. Need me to bring you some clothes?"

I look down at my sweaty shirt. "Yes, please. Whatever you think. And some deodorant. And some shoes to match whatever outfit you bring. And my makeup bag."

Sophie laughs. "Anything else?"

"If I could figure out how to squeeze a shower in I would."

"Yeah, not sure I can help with that. Call me if you think of anything else."

"Thanks, Soph! I couldn't do this without you."

We end the call and I make sure the ringer is off before dropping the phone back into the pocket of my shorts. I really look out of place here in these literal mom shorts and this shirt that isn't cute at all. The girls who are playing are decked out in Lululemon everything. The short skirt, the fitted sleeveless tank, the whole outfit. And each has a big bow or a visor. All perfectly color-coordinated. Right down to the golf shoes and socks that barely peek out.

I pace slowly behind all of the golfers, keeping an eye on the shrinking pyramids.

"Nice shot, Leo!" a guy yells.

Wait. He can be loud, but I get murder glares over my phone ringing? And then my brain snags on the name.

It can't be. It's a coincidence. And then he turns around.

I'm about to run the other way when I hear, "Olivia? Is that you?"

Crap. This can't be happening. So much for the family not finding out what I'm doing.

"Hey," I say, shoving the panic deep down at being caught. "Hey! What're you doing?"

What're you doing? Uh, he's playing golf. So dumb.

"Getting some practice in," he answers easily, as if I didn't just ask the most ridiculous question ever.

"Yes. Of course," I say.

The other guy goes back to practicing but Leo walks toward me, his golf club still in his hand. There's a bright green grip at the top, which sort of surprises me, but I don't know why.

A million things run through my head. *Please don't tell*

anyone I'm here! If you mention you saw me, you're a dead man. I'm not Olivia, but I get that all the time!

"I didn't know you'd be out here. Do you work here? No one mentioned it."

And there it is.

"Yeah, no one mentioned you'd be out here either," I say, ignoring his question. *But I would have prepared if they had! I would have been on a constant lookout for you.*

"Yeah, I'm playing in tomorrow's tournament. Hoping to get a spot on the LSU team for the fall."

He must be pretty good to even have a shot at an SEC school team. I don't know much about Leo since he moved away. Did he play golf before he left? No idea! All I know is he lives in Baton Rouge but still sees the Evil Joes on the regular, since there have been several holidays (minor ones like Memorial Day weekend and the Fourth of July) they've missed being with us because they were with Leo's family. I guess he's staying with Aunt Maggie Mae while he's in town for the tournament.

"Oh, good . . . Good luck. . . ." I fumble for something witty to say, but I really need to just get it over with. "Look, no one in the family knows I'm working here this week and I'd like to keep it that way, so would you please not mention it to anyone?"

One eyebrow rises, so I match him by raising one of mine. He smiles and his whole face brightens.

"Not even the other ones know?" he asks.

"What other ones?"

"The other ones in your little group." He squints as he looks up at the bright blue sky. "What does Mary Jo call y'all?"

I can't help flinching. "She has a name for us?" Which is the dumbest thing I can say or be surprised about because we have a name for ourselves—the Fab Four—but I'm sure that's not the one he's trying to think of. And we obviously have a name for the Evil Joes.

I can tell the second he remembers. "The Fake Four! That's it!"

Fake? How are we fake? "That's a stupid name," I say. Wait until I tell Charlie.

"So do any of the Fake Four know you're here?" he asks.

I raise that one eyebrow again. "Don't call us that." I wait a second before I continue. "And yes, Charlie, Sophie, and Wes know I'm here, but that's it."

He gets serious. "Why don't you want anyone to know you're here?" He looks around the course. "It's not a bad thing to be here."

I take a deep breath. "It's my business why I'm here, and it's important to me. Can we leave it at that?"

He studies me for a moment. "Sure. It will be our little secret."

Oh, I'm not sure I like the way he says *secret*.

"Excuse me," a golfer from down the line yells to me. "Where can I get some range balls?"

Half of the other golfers tell him to shut up.

"I gotta go," I say, and walk away before Leo can say anything else.

This is officially the worst day ever and it's only eight thirty a.m.

Phone Duty: Sophie

Charlie warned me Aunt Lisa would text a bunch, but it's no joke. Though I don't get why he was complaining so much. It's easy when you get the hang of it. Aunt Lisa likes to talk, and as long as you give her some sort of answer, she's all good. She's like my mom at warp speed. We've texted back and forth a few times and she was actually pretty helpful reminding me what I should bring for Olivia to wear to the party, since Olivia didn't leave any instructions. I had totally forgotten about that cute turquoise sundress she got when we were shopping in Dallas last month. Oh, and those gold hoop earrings will look great with it, especially if she pulls her hair up.

But then I remember there is a hat to go with this. Need to find the hat.

The dress is sleeveless, so I throw a razor in the bag in case she needs to shave under her arms. I'm as familiar with Olivia's room as I am with mine, which makes it easy to find all the things I'll need to bring her.

MOM: Those gold wedges would be adorable! Wear those!

Oh, good call, Aunt Lisa. Those would look perfect!

I type, Yes! Those will look great! But delete it since that is way too perky for Olivia. So instead I type: Ok

Olivia's phone keeps vibrating, and I can see a group text she's on is going a little nuts. I take a moment to check if there's anything she needs to be aware of, but it's really just a lot of messages flying back and forth about what everyone is wearing. Should I respond for her? Is that crossing the line? I recognize several names in the group, but it feels wrong to text them as if I'm Olivia. They'll just have to wonder why she's not responding.

It's really weird handling someone else's communications. Olivia has already forwarded me a few messages from my friend Addie back in Minden and one from Wes because he forgot I switched phones for the day. I get why she didn't ask one of her friends she goes to school with to answer these texts. There are very few people I would trust getting a peek into my life like this.

Hmm. Maybe I should have deleted my conversation with Wes before I gave my phone to Olivia. I'll never hear the end of it if she scrolls through our messages. I can feel myself blush just thinking about it.

I put everything in a bag and head for my car, making sure to lock up before I leave and drop the key back under the mat. Wes sent me directions to the bed-and-breakfast where the party is taking place, and I leave in plenty of time to get there in case I get turned around. It's actually not very far from Olivia's house.

By the time I arrive, I've felt Olivia's phone vibrate several times. That group chat is really blowing up. I pull her phone out of my purse to see if she's missing something big, but it's her mom.

MOM: Make sure you say hello to Mrs. Woods and thank her for having you! She's one of the hostesses and she's in my bunco group and has been talking about this party for months!
ME: Yes ma'am!

I hit SEND before I can take back that exclamation point. Oh, well. Maybe Aunt Lisa will think Olivia is in a very good mood today. I can't forget to tell Olivia she has to make a point to speak to Mrs. Woods when she gets here.

Exiting out of Aunt Lisa's convo, I see there is a new unread message. I open it up.

UNKNOWN NUMBER: I don't know where you went but they are looking for you

Oh no. I call my phone immediately. Olivia answers on the first ring.

"I'm halfway there! Sorry! It was harder to sneak away than I thought it would be," she says. She sounds flustered. Or out of breath.

"You need to turn around, I think," I say. "Someone just texted and said they were looking for you."

"What?" she screeches. "Who is it?"

"I don't know. You don't have their contact in your phone. Want me to ask?"

"No!" she answers quickly. "Coach gave my number to all the players from my school, but Locke's was the only one I didn't already have. It's probably him. But ignore him—don't text back." I can almost hear the screech of tires as she turns around. "I guess I'm missing the luncheon."

Oh crap!

"Wait! Your mom wants you to say hello to Mrs. Woods! I already responded to her that you would."

We both let out a groan.

"You'll have to go in there. Be me. She won't know the difference," Olivia says.

"Are you kidding me?" My voice comes out in a very high pitch that I barely recognize. "I mean, we look like we're related, but that's it. Anyone who knows you would know I'm not you."

"Well, I can't get there and we can't fall apart on day one!" she says. "I haven't seen Mrs. Woods in years. Literally years. You and I are the same height, same dark hair, same build. Plus, you'll be wearing a hat. I swear she won't know. You can do this!"

And as I start digging out the turquoise dress I packed for her, I remember she's the master of talking me into dumb ideas. I crawl into the backseat while Olivia continues her pep talk over Bluetooth.

"Go in, find Mrs. Woods, say hi, and get out of there. I'll send you a pic of her from Facebook so you'll know which mom she is. They invited a ton of girls, so you'll blend right in and they won't miss you when you leave."

"I can't believe I'm doing this," I mumble. I slip the dress on and wiggle out of my shorts. I strap on the shoes and run my fingers through my hair before putting the hat on.

"Go ahead and get in there, since you're early. You'll run into fewer people that way. Okay, I'm back at the golf course. Call me once you're done. I love you!"

And then she's gone.

"I cannot be-*lieve* I'm about to walk into this party and act like I'm her," I say to absolutely no one but myself. "This is the dumbest, stupidest, most ridiculous thing she has ever asked me to do. And I'm doing it."

I get out through the backseat and half walk/half run up the driveway to the bed-and-breakfast, holding on to the hat so it doesn't blow away. A quick glance shows there are only a few cars, so maybe Olivia is right. I can get in and get out. The house is three stories and painted a bright blue that would be ugly if this were actually your house but somehow works as a B&B. The windows are trimmed in white and there's a wrap-around porch with hanging ferns between each post. I decide against the front door and walk through the yard toward the side door. I feel like I need to know what I'm getting into before I'm in it.

The door squeaks when I open it, and I peek inside. There are four moms fluffing flowers and arranging food on trays. Their chatter bounces around the room, and I wonder how they can actually follow along with everyone talking at once. Taking a second to check the pic Olivia just sent of Mrs. Woods, I see she's blond and thin with very straight hair that hits right at her shoulders. I peek inside the room again, and great, she looks exactly like the other three moms here.

I step back out and gently close the door. I move to the side of the building and FaceTime Wes.

"Hey, what's up?" he says once the call connects. "You look cute in a hat!"

Awww! "You're pretty cute yourself!"

And then I remember where I am and what I'm doing.

"I'm freaking out!" I whisper-scream. My face is so close to the screen that I'm sure he can see up my nose. "Olivia can't make it and I have to go in and say hi to some woman named Mrs. Woods because Aunt Lisa said to and Olivia thinks this Mrs. Woods won't know it's not her but, come on, of course she'll know I'm not her but there are four moms in that room and I don't know which one she is and if the others would know Olivia on sight and did I tell you I'm freaking out." I finish and have to drag in a deep breath.

"Okay, it's going to be okay. Don't panic," he whispers back. "Can you point the phone in the direction of the moms? I played soccer a few years ago with her son. I think I can pick her out."

I tiptoe back to the door and open it just enough to hold the phone up. I give him four full seconds before I pull it back.

"Did you see her?"

And there's that big smile I love so much. "Yeah, she's in the yellow dress. The other moms will definitely know Olivia, so steer clear of them. Wait until Mrs. Woods is alone, and you'll be fine. She's kind of clueless, so Olivia's right, she probably won't know you from her."

I kiss the screen and promise to call him as soon as I'm done. I need to get my bearings and see if there's a better way in where I can single out Mrs. Woods, so I walk around to the back of the bed-and-breakfast, stopping in front of a white wooden gate set into a brick wall. Peeking through the slats, I see the party is set up back here. It's like a secret garden.

Small trees, flowering plants, and creeping vines flank an old brick path that leads to a fountain in the center. There is a long table set to the side with three huge flower arrangements in big vases—one on each end and one in the middle. I zoom in and get the pictures I know Aunt Lisa will ask for later. Round tables are scattered through the space, each with smaller versions of the main arrangements. I get pics of those, too.

I'm determined to be the best Olivia.

The moms come from inside the house bearing trays of food they take extra care to arrange on the long table. There's no yellow dress in the mix, so I run back to the side door, hoping to catch Mrs. Woods alone while I have the chance.

I throw open the door and head straight to her.

"Hi!" I say, more loudly than I mean to.

She jumps, but then she gives me a gigantic smile and it's clear she has no idea who I am. So here goes nothing.

"I'm Olivia . . ."

"Yes, of course! Lisa's daughter. You are her spitting image!" Our moms are twins, so I guess that makes sense? Now she's beaming and coming at me with outstretched arms.

"Thank you so much for inviting me! Everything looks beautiful."

She pulls me in for a hug, but it's the kind that still maintains a little distance so as not to knock off our hats or mess up our makeup. "We're so glad to have you. Sarah is upstairs and should be down any second." And then she lets go and turns back to the tray of croissants fresh from the oven. My mouth waters just looking at them. "Go make yourself at home. Grab some punch!"

Now I'm stuck. I can't turn back around and walk out. But I can't go out to the courtyard because then I'll have to speak to the woman who will know for sure I'm not Olivia.

"I need a bathroom," I say. Smooth.

Mrs. Woods points down a narrow hall. "Any one of these bedrooms has a bathroom. Take your pick!"

And off I go. I find the bedroom farthest away and lock the door once I'm inside. I call Wes back.

"Did you make it out alive?" he says as soon as he answers.

"No!" I'm back to whisper-shouting. "I'm trapped in this bedroom. I spoke to Mrs. Woods but then I panicked."

I'm pacing the room. And sweating. Sweating like a common criminal! I should have used the deodorant I brought for Olivia.

"Just turn around and walk out. I promise you are overthinking this. No one will say anything. Just walk out."

"Of course I'm overthinking it! But it doesn't help knowing it and I can't stop." I pause in front of one of the windows. "I'm crawling out of the window."

"What?" he yells. "Soph, just walk through the door. Any door."

I'm shaking my head. "Nope. I can't go back out there. I'll call you back." I end the call and shove Olivia's phone into my bra, since this dress doesn't have pockets and I'm going to need both hands. Pushing the drapes apart, I open the window and let out a breath of relief when I realize it faces the front porch. I run back to the door and unlock it but keep it closed. Then I'm back at the window and throw one leg out. God, if anyone saw me right now I don't know how I would explain this.

Sophie Patrick, Tea Party Crasher and Escapee.

I try to pull the other leg through, but my wedge gets caught on the windowsill and I end up exiting headfirst. My hat rolls across the porch. I look up to see three girls standing in front of what is probably the main entrance.

"Are you okay?" one of the girls asks. I'm sure I exposed myself in some way when my dress flew up, but I can't worry about that right now.

I don't recognize any of them, which is good. "Yes, I'm so clumsy. Sorry. I got locked in that room, trying to find a bathroom."

They think I'm losing it, but at least they don't ask me any questions. The girl closest to the door reaches for the doorbell and I know I've got to get out of here before that door opens or I'm right back where I started.

I speed-walk past them, grabbing my hat as I go down the

front steps and around the corner. I hear one of them say, "Who was that?" and another one answer, "I have no idea, but *love* her shoes."

I don't relax until I'm back in my car. Olivia's phone rings from inside my bra and I jump in my seat. It's Wes.

"Are you okay?" he says as soon as the call connects.

"Yes, I'm out. And I'm never doing that again."

He laughs for so long I almost hang up on him. Finally he says, "Come meet me for lunch. I want to hear all about it."

"I can't! I'm Olivia, remember? I have to sit here until the party's over, or Aunt Lisa will know."

"Okay, I'll pick up some food and come to you. Picnic in your car?"

"Yes! Croissants if you can find them!"

Olivia

I've only been gone from Ellerbe Hills for about nine minutes, but it feels like hours. Or maybe I've lost all concept of time, since I feel like I live here now.

When I left, the players had teed off and were playing a round just like they will tomorrow when it counts. I've fetched for them, replenished snacks and water, found batteries for devices I don't even recognize, so what could Coach possibly want from me now?

At least the guard at the entrance recognizes me and waves me through.

I park in the far corner in case Coach is close by, so he won't see me getting out of my car. I have to hustle to cross the parking lot, but it only takes me a few minutes to get past the clubhouse and out onto the course. And sure enough, there is Coach Cantu, hand shading his eyes from the sun overhead, searching for me.

He looks frustrated when he finally spots me. "Olivia, I need you to take a cart and this box of flagging." The box is full of small red flags on metal stakes. He points to the green that's closest to us. "See how I put those flags in the ground on the edge of the cart path next to the green? You know what the green is, right? The section with the really short grass right around the hole?"

I nod, trying not to be embarrassed by how little he thinks I understand the game. I mean, I know what the green is, but other than that he's not far off.

"I need you to set these flags beside the cart path at each green to keep the parents out of the action. They always try to get too close, but hopefully this will help."

"Every couple of feet?"

"Yes, just next to the path when it gets close to the green."

I thought golf was all about quiet and not disrupting anyone, but I'll be flying from spot to spot if I'm supposed to do this throughout the entire course before midnight.

"Keep to the cart path. Stay still if you come up to someone teeing off," Coach says as if he can read my mind, then hands me a walkie-talkie. "Keep this on the lowest volume setting. This way I can let you know if I need you."

He won't carry a phone, but he'll carry a walkie-talkie. And now there's never going to be a chance for me to leave the grounds if he can call me on this.

Coach Cantu puts an ice chest in the back of my cart along with a bag full of extra snacks, paper towels, and a stack of washcloths.

"The cold snacks are in the chest with water and Gatorades," he says. "The washrags can be soaked in the watered-down ice if one of the players is getting overheated. There's also a first aid kit back here. Call me if you need anything."

He waves his walkie-talkie at me, then heads back to the clubhouse. It takes me longer than it should to get the hang of the golf cart. The slightest tap to the gas has me shooting off, and the same small tap on the brake almost throws me through the nonexistent front windshield. And don't get me started on the high-pitched whining noise that draws every eye to me when I put the cart in reverse.

The front and back nine holes basically start in the same

general area, then head in opposite directions. I decide to go in numerical order, so hole one's up first. From what I can tell, there are both lots of tournament players practicing today and a lot of random golfers getting in a game before the course is closed to anyone who isn't playing in the tournament the rest of the week. It's easy to tell who's who, since there is about a forty-year age gap between the two groups.

I drive fast when there's no one around, then take it slow and easy when I get near anyone. People are playing everywhere, and I don't want to mess anyone up. There are several carts on the path driven by what must be a few of the players' parents. Some of them are videoing their kids, while others are calling out tips, but the one who is quickly becoming my least favorite is the dad literally berating his daughter every time she hits the ball in a way he doesn't like.

"Sierra, you shanked it! It's like you're not even listening to me!"

And somehow Sierra doesn't react to him at all. She puts the club she just finished using back into the bag and heads toward where her ball landed.

"Freddy, you have got to stop yelling at her," a woman from another cart says. "They'll kick you out of here just like last time."

Freddy bangs his hand on the top of the steering wheel. "I swear to God she's doing it on purpose. Does she not know how important this tournament is?"

Does he not know how awful he is? I pull slightly off the path so I can get around them and then speed away.

Each hole is different. On some, there's a long stretch to flag as the cart path snakes around, but on others, it's only a few feet.

I find the guys from my school on hole four. There are a few parents following behind them, too, but none as loud as Sierra's dad. And I finally feel useful when Cal and David both need waters. Just as they walk back to their bags, Locke heads in my direction.

"Hey! Need a drink? A snack?" I'm trying to be extra nice, since he gave me a heads-up about Coach looking for me, but it's wasted on him.

"No, but do you have any Advil in there?"

I turn around and grab the first aid kit. It takes some digging, but I finally pull out a small bottle. "How many you want?" I ask.

"Give me four," he says.

That's probably over the recommended dosage, but I just give him what he asks for. "Anything else?" I ask after he throws the pills back and chases them with some water.

"Are you going to be here all week?" he asks.

I shrug. "I guess. It's up to Coach." Even though I know I will be.

He's quiet a second, then says, "Most of us here need to

do well. Especially those of us graduating. Just don't make it harder than it already is."

And then he's gone.

What was that about? Am I screwing up his game in some way I'm unaware of? Was taking twenty seconds to text me that Coach was looking for me enough to ruin his whole day?

I get back in my cart and drive off to the next hole. I'm not sure I can take a week of this.

Truth #5: Not all togas are created equal

Tuesday, May 10ᵗʰ, Afternoon

Phone Duty: Sophie

"I wish I could have seen you fall out of that window," Wes says in a low voice.

He laughs and I give him a shove in the side, which only makes him laugh harder.

"I'm sure I flashed those poor girls. At least they didn't know who I was."

"Not gonna lie, I'm a little worried about my day tomorrow," Charlie says.

Yeah, we're all worried about Charlie's day tomorrow.

We're at Nonna's, hanging out in her kitchen, eating strawberry pie. I'm still "Olivia," fielding texts from her mom and her friends asking where she is. And because she didn't sign out of her social media apps, I'm getting messages from every direction.

I'm only answering Aunt Lisa at this point, but the notifications are piling up.

"Should I answer Bailey and Mia?" I ask Wes and Charlie. "They keep texting."

Wes shrugs and gives me an *I have no idea* look. "Maybe if you keep it simple?"

I decide to only respond to texts. Olivia can go through the other apps later.

I type Sorry I missed it! It looked so beautiful! Got caught up helping my grandmother at work! just as Charlie adds, "But chill with the exclamation points. You're way more upbeat than Olivia and it shows."

And now I'm editing the message. I hate it when he's right. I send the message then see another new one that just came in.

"This is the second message she's gotten from this number. Olivia says it's from some guy named Locke," I say.

Both of them swing their heads toward me.

"Let me see," Charlie says.

I hold her phone close. "Maybe she doesn't want you to see?" I say.

Charlie's forehead scrunches in confusion. "I'll see tomorrow when I have her phone ALL DAY LONG." And then he's pulling it from me.

Charlie reads the message out loud: "'I'm sorry. Didn't mean to be an ass earlier. Hope you didn't get in trouble.'"

"Whoa, why was he an ass?" Wes says.

"Should we reply?" Charlie asks. "Tell him to go to—"

"No!" I say before he finishes. "He's apologizing. Maybe he's just stressed out?"

"Locke is pretty intense. Eats, sleeps, and breathes golf." Wes reads the text again.

Charlie shrugs. "I don't really know him."

"Because he's always playing golf," Wes replies.

Charlie is about to say something else but stops when we hear Nonna in the hall. She's usually at the shop this time of the day, but she took the afternoon off to meet a plumber for a leaky sink in one of the upstairs bathrooms.

"I picked up those little picture frames I was telling you about. We'll put their senior pictures in them. It will look so cute on the entrance table," she says loudly.

I pop my head around the corner to see if she's talking to us, but she's sorting the mail, her phone on the hall table.

And then I hear Aunt Lisa's voice come over the speaker. "Oh, perfect, Mom. I've got the pictures at my house. Had them printed before I left. Why don't you go ahead and give the frames to Olivia and tell her to put them on my desk in the office."

I spin back around and look at Wes and Charlie, matching expressions of panic on all of our faces.

"I'll give it to her when I see her, but she hasn't been here today," Nonna says.

"Huh. That's weird. It says she's there," Aunt Lisa says.

Charlie holds up Olivia's phone, then sprints like lightning out of the back door.

"What says she's here?" Nonna asks, her footsteps getting closer. She peeks into the kitchen as if she's looking for some foreign device.

"Her phone. It's an app. It says she's there," Aunt Lisa says.

Wes and I turn to face Nonna and she's looking at us.

"Is Olivia here?" she asks us.

I open my mouth to say something, but I go blank and no words come out. Wes is quicker on his feet.

"She was here. Ran in for a sec while you were upstairs. But she just left with Charlie."

Nonna has that look like she knows we're lying. It's the kind of look that makes you squirm. I concentrate really hard on not squirming.

"Uh-huh," she says, still piercing us with her stare.

"I can take the frames to her house, Nonna," I say, finally finding my voice.

Her head tilts. "It's okay. I'll give them to her later."

Nonna has gotten a whiff that something is up. This does not bode well for us. With a parting glance, she leaves the room, her conversation with Aunt Lisa resuming.

"Looks like she's back at our house," Aunt Lisa says.

Wes and I wash and put up our plates with record speed. We've got to get to Olivia's and make sure Charlie doesn't say something dumb to Aunt Lisa.

Olivia

I'm sunburned, I'm exhausted, and I'm pretty sure I pulled something. Today was rough. And I have three more days to go.

I'm lying on the floor in our den with the ceiling fan on high when Charlie races inside followed quickly by Sophie and Wes. Charlie pokes me with his foot.

"Is she dead?" he asks.

I raise one hand and flip him off.

"Nope!" he says. "Good as ever!"

Sophie plops onto the floor next to me and I can see her hand hovering over my arm in my peripheral vision.

"That looks like it hurts," she says. I know she's dying to poke my skin to see just how burned I am.

"I'm on fire," I answer.

She jumps up as quickly as she sat down. "Nonna will have something for this! I'll be right back." And then she's gone.

Charlie and Wes sit on the couch right behind me.

"Tough day on the course?" Wes asks.

I raise my hand and flip him off, too. They both laugh.

"Nonna may be onto us," Charlie says. "She was talking to your mom when 'you' were at her house." He puts *you* in finger quotes.

This has me sitting up. "What happened?"

Wes waves me off. "We handled it. We were brilliant."

"Brilliant enough that Nonna may be onto us?"

They both look at each other then back to me. "Well, you know how she just *knows* everything, right?" Wes says.

"Okay, so maybe y'all steer clear of her house," I say.

Charlie looks offended. "But that's where the pie is."

It doesn't take long for Sophie to get back with cream to put on my arms and legs. I'm sure we would have all perished years ago if Nonna wasn't a couple of blocks away.

"You really should shower first and then put this on," she says, then turns to the guys. "We're heading up to get dressed. Want to meet us back here for the party?"

"Yeah, that works," Wes says as he gets up from the couch.

"I'm not sure I can get off the floor," I say at the exact same time.

"You're going. At this rate, this may be the last grad party you make," Charlie says. Then he adds, "Get Sophie to tell you how she fell out of a window today."

Sophie rolls her eyes. "I tripped."

"You fell out of a window?" I shriek. "Please tell me it wasn't at that tea party."

Sophie helps me up. "I'll tell you all about it while we're getting ready."

An hour later, we're heading back downstairs and I can tell Sophie is having a hard time not laughing. While I'm totally fried from the elbows down, my tan skin looks pale in comparison from the elbows up, including the one bare shoulder. Except for my neck and face. Those parts are red as well. And the burn seems especially red and the skin especially pale against the stark white of a toga.

It's . . . not a good look.

I hold my arms out in front of me. I don't want to miss tonight's party, especially since I missed Sarah's tea today, but this is ridiculous. "I don't know if I can show up like this."

"It's not that bad," Sophie tries to assure me between giggles. "I promise."

But when Wes and Charlie get here, I know it definitely is that bad. They can barely keep themselves from crying, they're laughing so hard.

Charlie holds up the edge of his red polka-dotted sheet. "Maybe we should trade! You could blend in a little better with this one."

"Let's go before I change my mind," I say as I walk past him to his truck.

It's a twenty-minute drive to the party. I'm riding shotgun while Wes and Sophie are in the backseat.

"There isn't a party tomorrow night, is there?" Wes asks.

"No, thank God," I say, and then hate how grumpy I sound. This is supposed to be the best week of high school and I'm miserable.

"No, why?" Charlie asks.

"Judd joined a band," he says. There's a pause, and then we all crack up.

Sophie chokes out, "I hope he's not the singer!" We've all had the unfortunate experience of listening to Judd sing karaoke.

"Nah, he's on the drums," Wes answers.

Charlie glances back at Wes in the rearview mirror. "Since when has Judd played the drums?"

I turn around in my seat and see Wes just shrug. "No idea. But they have their first gig tomorrow night at Superior. I told him we'd come by and watch them play."

"Oh yeah, not missing that," I say, laughing. Then I cringe because all this movement is making the burn on my face hurt.

We finally arrive at our destination. It's a monstrosity of a house in one of the nicest gated neighborhoods in town. There are six different families throwing the party honoring four guys, so it's big. Like over-the-top enormous.

Charlie pulls up to the house and there's a valet there, ready to whisk his truck away.

"I don't know how I feel about this." Charlie holds his door closed while he and the valet have a staring contest through the closed window. "No one drives this truck but me."

We pile out, leaving Charlie alone in the truck. He finally gives in but watches until it's out of sight.

There's a pair of guys in white togas—real-looking ones, not the kind made out of sheets—off to the side next to two big white freestanding columns.

"Party's this way," one of them says, pointing us down a path lined with more columns, each pair about twenty feet apart.

Charlie steps closer to one of them and asks, "How'd y'all get this gig? And what's it pay an hour?"

They ignore him.

Just as we're about to take off down the path, a car pulls up. I glance back and see it's the golfers from our school who practiced today.

"Oh God," I say. They spent the same amount of time in the sun as I did, yet none of them looks like a crispy critter.

"What? Who is it?" Sophie says.

"It's Locke," Charlie says, but drags his name out in a weird way.

I turn around and look at him. "Why do you say it like that?"

"I didn't think you could blush with a sunburn, but you

can!" Wes and Charlie high-five, thinking they are hilarious. Sophie and I punch them.

"He texted you today. Apologized for being mean," Sophie whispers since they're walking this way. "I didn't respond because I didn't know if his apology should be accepted."

She told me I got a lot of texts, but I haven't gone back through and actually looked at them yet.

"Hey," Lily says when they get close. And then she winces when she sees the sunburn. "Oh no, you forgot sunblock."

And I know this will be the one thing *everyone* will comment on tonight.

"Yep," I answer. "I'm surprised y'all are here."

Most of the guys don't look happy about it.

Em Beth pipes up, "We forced them. All they care about is golf, and it's no fun to miss every single senior party, so they agreed to make an appearance."

"One hour," Locke says.

"You seemed to be okay with being at the Wagon Wheel last night." I told myself I wasn't going to talk to Locke anymore, but here I am.

"That was the night before practice. Not the night before a match."

Lily pulls David, and Em Beth latches on to Cal as she says, "Well, we shouldn't waste a single second, then."

Locke is slower to walk away. I can tell he has something

else to say, but he eyes Wes, Sophie, and Charlie, clearly not wanting an audience. Finally, he follows his friends.

Sophie claps. "Oh, he was giving you eyes!"

"Eyes. What does that mean?" Charlie is clearly confused.

Sophie's face scrunches up. "Eyes. Like he couldn't quit looking at her. Love eyes. Heart eyes."

"You're seeing something that isn't there," I say.

We give their group a head start, then follow them down the column-lined path, which wraps around the back of the house. There is a pool in the middle of the yard and more white columns, along with small fire pits sprinkled throughout the space. It's like something you'd see on TV.

There are already of lot of people here and quite a few like Charlie who decided to forgo the traditional white sheet for something more entertaining. There's a guy wearing a *Star Wars* sheet and carrying a lightsaber and a group of girls decked out as every color in the rainbow. We stick together and circulate through the crowd, finding people we know.

Ross, one of the honorees, joins us, giving Wes and Charlie fist bumps. "Y'all made it!"

"This is insane!" Wes says.

Sophie and I are both just trying to take everything in.

"My wedding reception won't be this nice," Sophie leans near me to say.

"Yeah, mine either."

There is a tent with food on the other side of the pool and a band toward the back, getting ready to play.

"Food that way," Ross says, pointing toward the tent. "And there's a keg hidden behind those bushes," he adds, pointing in the opposite direction, then he moves on to greet another group of people who just got here.

Charlie spots Bianca and off he goes, while Wes and Sophie head toward Judd, who is already on the dance floor. I make my way to where Bailey and Mia are hanging out.

Their faces are identical when they see my sunburn.

"That looks painful!" Mia says.

"So painful," I agree.

Yep, main topic of conversation.

The sky is just getting dark and the fire pits everywhere are throwing off a pretty cool glow. People are pouring in now, and it's obvious most have discovered the keg in the bushes.

"It sucks you had to work today. You missed what happened at Sarah's party!" Bailey says.

Sophie told me about the excuse she texted them. Now I'm in the awkward place of not being able to tell them what I'm doing this week because then I'll have to admit Sophie was pretending to be me on the phone and lied to them. There's already tension now that Sophie is here all the time, and it just feels like I'm too far down this hole right now. My mom used to repeat this dumb saying to my brother all the time (usually when he got busted trying to lie to her): *Oh, what a tangled web we weave, when first we practice to deceive.* It's embarrassing that it now applies to me.

"What happened?" I ask. Part of me is scared they're going to tell the story of Sophie falling out of the front window.

"Mrs. Woods leaned forward to grab a tea sandwich off a tray and the feathers on her hat caught fire from one of the centerpiece candles," Mia says. "Three people threw their tea on her to put her out!"

They're laughing reliving it and I'm laughing picturing it. Really hard. I'm sorry I missed that.

Something behind me catches Bailey's attention. "Who's the cute guy with Mary Jo and Jo Lynn?"

I spin around and see the Evil Joes strutting in. Their togas are short and fitted and made out of some shiny fabric that practically glows. Of course, Aunt Maggie Mae probably had them specially made.

"Yeah, who's the hot friend?" Mia asks.

I let out a squeak and push Bailey in front of me. As I peek over her shoulder, there's Leo following the twins. And he looks really good in a toga.

Like ridiculously good. Who knew all those muscles were hiding under those golf shirts.

"That's Leo Perez. Do y'all remember him?"

"That's Leo?" they both repeat in unison.

It's like speaking his name somehow caught his attention

even though he's nowhere near us. His eyes land on the three of us and he excuses himself from the Evil Joes and heads this way.

"He's coming over here," Mia says, a little breathless.

But he's not the only one. When the Evil Joes catch on to where he's headed, they pivot and follow him.

Great.

Leo and I barely get along when the Evil Joes aren't around. I can't imagine it will be any better when they are. And what if he mentions seeing me today? Maybe he didn't take me seriously when I asked him to keep it a secret.

So I panic. "Where's the bathroom?" I ask Bailey.

She looks from me to Leo and back again, then points toward the house. "Inside."

And I'm all but running away. I can't get stuck talking to Leo in front of them, especially with the Evil Joes hot on his trail.

Instead of going inside, though, I spot a staircase tucked away on the edge of the porch that leads to a balcony. It's dark; I'm sure whoever owns this house doesn't want this space discovered so the party doesn't move up here. I take the steps two at a time, nearly tripping twice on my toga.

There are a few chairs up here and a perfect view of the party below. I find Leo immediately—he's talking to Mia and Bailey. The Joes are moving toward the keg in the bushes. Scanning the crowd, I see the golf group, which reminds me of the text Sophie said Locke sent. Pulling my phone out of the waistband of the shorts I'm wearing under this sheet, I open up his message and save his contact under *Locke*. As I read both of the messages, I try to figure out how it makes me feel. Should I text back? Will it be weird that I'm responding after I just saw him? Maybe this is why he was trying to talk to me earlier.

I decide to go for it.

ME: Thank you for apologizing and thank you for the heads up. You saved me from getting in trouble.

I look down to where he's standing, waiting for him to pull his phone out and read my message. He doesn't move. It's loud down there and anyway his phone is probably on silent.

Leo finally moves on from Bailey and Mia and I feel like it's safe to head back down. I'm determined to enjoy myself even though it feels like I'm navigating a minefield.

"You missed him!" Bailey says when I join them again.

"He asked where you ran off to," Mia teases, as if she knows I'm actively avoiding him.

I shake it off. "He's been at Nonna's a few times since he came to town and we've butted heads over the . . . uh . . . Mary Jo and Jo Lynn."

"C'mon, let's move closer to the band. The guy playing guitar is hot." Bailey pulls Mia and me to the dance floor.

Bailey picks a spot that's close to where Wes and Sophie are, and it's fun to dance with all of them at the same time. It's not long before Judd is down on the ground and the crowd has formed a circle around him. He's trying to do some sort of back spin move but he gets all tangled up in his toga. It only takes a rotation or two before his sheet splits open and tears away. When he pops back up, he's in a pair of boxers with orange and red flames all over them and the gold braided belt that once secured the toga.

He could care less and climbs onto the stage to play air guitar with the band. Someone should find a way to bottle that level of confidence.

The band is good, and we dance for a few songs. I track Leo on the other side of the yard, where he's hanging with the Evil Joes and some of the guys he was friends with when he lived here. Mary Jo says something, and then they're all laughing. I mean really laughing. Like about to fall out of their chairs howling, and it bothers me that he could be so entertained by her.

"I need a little air," I tell Mia, and sidestep my way through the crowd.

I sink into a chair on the patio. The day's exhaustion settles over me and I can't shake it. I'm ready to go home.

I search the crowd and find Charlie sitting next to Bianca, and from the body language, neither of them is ready to walk away. Wes and Sophie are hanging with a group near the band that includes Mia and Bailey. Sophie may not know many people here, and I hate to pull her away when she's having so much fun—especially when everyone seems to be getting along. There's no reason for any of them to leave just because I'm ready.

Opening the Uber app, I order a ride, then text Charlie, Olivia, and Wes.

ME: This sunburn is killing me and I'm exhausted from today. Uber is on the way.

CHARLIE: No wait I'll take you

WES: We can all go

SOPHIE: I barely know anyone here anyway

ME: No y'all stay. I'm just going to crash when I get home and that's no fun

ME: Seriously, I'm good

ME: Uber is almost here

They all double- and triple-check with me, but I hold strong. My ride is only a few minutes away, so I pick up my drooping toga and head toward the front of the house.

"Olivia!"

I freeze. That's Leo's voice.

He catches up with me and I say, "Hey," then look around to see if the Evil Joes are about to jump out of the shrubbery.

He gives me a big smile like he didn't just call us the Fake Four a few hours ago. Then his gaze zeroes in on my sunburn, just like everyone else, but I stop him before he can say anything.

"I know, I'm burned. It looks horrible, but it's fine." I start walking again.

"Are you leaving?" His voice should be farther away, but it's not.

Glancing back over my shoulder, I notice he's following me. "Yeah, I have to be back out there early and I'm exhausted."

"Yeah, me too. Mae wanted me to come with the girls even though I told her I was wiped. It's hard to say no to her."

Oh, I know.

It's so weird to hear him refer to Aunt Maggie Mae as *Mae* and the Evil Joes as *the girls*. "She lets you call her Mae?" I ask before I can stop myself. "She's always made a big deal to the family that her name is Maggie Mae and shouldn't be shortened."

His long legs close the gap between us and now we're walking side by side back through the row of columns.

"I had a speech impediment when I was little. A stutter. I tried to call her Mrs. Messina but got tripped up on the *m*'s and *s*'s, so she told me to call her Mae. It just stuck."

God, he makes them almost sound normal.

Time to change the subject. "Are you nervous about tomorrow?"

"Yeah. I've got a lot riding on this." He turns toward me, his face solemn. "Just like everybody else out there."

We stop near the valet stand but wave them off when they ask us for our ticket.

"How are you getting to the Ev . . ." I stop myself before I say *Evil Joes.* "To Aunt Maggie Mae's?"

"Oh," he says, pulling his phone out of some hidden place under his sheet. "I was going to get an Uber. But I got distracted." He gives me a quick smile before looking back at his phone.

And now I'm probably blushing again. At least Charlie and Wes aren't here to point it out. "You can ride with me. And then I can drive you to Aunt Maggie Mae's. I mean, we're both basically going to the same place. It's dumb to get two Ubers."

He agrees quickly. "Yeah, that'd be great. But I can walk from your place. It's not far."

I check the app to see how close the car is because now it's a little bit awkward with just us and the two valet guys out here.

"I'd be lying if I said it wasn't driving me nuts that I'm keeping your secret but I don't know why." His voice is a near whisper.

My eyes stay glued to my phone. "I'm okay with you lying." I have a smirk. I can feel it. I cannot make it go away.

I'm relieved when the car pulls into the driveway, though it's a tiny little four-door and we are squished in the backseat together.

The driver is not talking and neither are we, and this

awkwardness is worse than the one we had going on a few minutes ago.

"Is working the golf tournament a secret from your whole family or just the girls?" he asks.

I take a deep breath. "Everyone." I hate saying it out loud. "But especially them."

"Why do you think y'all don't get along with Jo Lynn and Mary Jo?" he finally asks.

Our track record isn't good when it comes to talking about them, but apparently we're going there.

"Because they're mean?"

He lifts his shoulders and nods his head as if he's really weighing my answer. "I think they think y'all are the mean ones," he finally says. "You don't know them like I do."

I try to spin around to face him, but it's so tight in the backseat I end up knocking my knees against his.

"They were mean long before we were. Like when we were little. We only take up for ourselves."

"I was around back then, so it's not like I don't know how it was."

This has me gasping for words. "What? Are you serious? I know you're close to them, but you're blind where they are concerned. If you only knew what they did to Sophie this past Christmas!"

His face scrunches up. "Are we talking about the movie date again?"

"It was drive-in porn!"

We pitch forward when the driver taps the brakes. We both look at him and he's staring at us in his rearview mirror. "There's a drive-in that shows porn here?"

My face scrunches up. "Ew."

Leo shakes his head. "There's no way they knew that's where he was taking her."

And now my eyes are bugging out. "You are so gullible!"

"I'm just saying, there are two sides and I don't think you ever consider theirs."

I'm muttering *no, no no* before he even finishes his sentence. "You were just as bad when you lived here. Bad as them. You tried to beat Charlie up."

He barks out something between a laugh and growl. Too loud for this tiny car. "Are you talking about when we were at the park for that school party?"

I won't look at him. "You know exactly when I'm talking about."

"Charlie had run into both of them like three times before he finally knocked Jo Lynn over," Leo argues. "Is that why he's been looking at me like he wants to go another round?"

"They were playing football. And Jo Lynn was practically in the middle of their game hoping one of those boys would notice her. And no, Charlie is completely over it," I lie.

He starts to say something—I'm sure something in their defense—but I stop him. "We're not talking about this."

"So that's two subjects off the table," he mumbles. He leans forward just an inch. "What *can* we talk about?"

I open my mouth to say something but nothing comes out. We are far too close together in the backseat of this car. Is it hot in here?

Turning to stare out of the side window, I hear him chuckle at his small victory that I had to look away first. Neither of us says anything else until we get to my house.

We unfold ourselves out of the car and watch the Uber drive off. "How much for the ride?" Leo asks.

"I got it," I say, waving him off.

"I guess I'll see you tomorrow, then." We're on the curb in front of my house.

"I can drive you."

He doesn't really look at me. "I can walk. It's not far." He takes a few steps, then stops. Turning back, he says, "I hate that I wasted the ride fighting with you."

Before I can even think of how to respond to that, he starts back down the sidewalk in the direction of the Evil Joes' house. I don't know what it means that I stay in the same spot until he's no longer in sight.

He never looked back once.

I drag myself inside and take another shower, hoping it will get me out of this funk. When I'm about to climb into my bed, I notice my phone has a screen full of notifications. I open the one from Mom first.

MOM: Aw, it looks like you left the party early? Was it not fun? Loved the pic you sent of the four of y'all in your togas! But why are you so sunburnt like that? I thought your dress you wore today was sleeveless.

ME: I changed into a t-shirt and shorts after the luncheon and sat outside with Sophie. Didn't realize how long we were out there

Next, I open up the group message I have with Sophie, Wes, and Charlie.

SOPHIE: Just making sure you made it home!

ME: Yes! Showered and about to get in bed. Y'all have fun

And then I see Locke finally texted me back.

LOCKE: Let's start over. No talk about MJ or JL or Charlie. No questions asked about why you're at the course. Deal?

Oh crap. My stomach flips. This isn't Locke. And if he's mentioning MJ and JL, there's really only one other person this can be.

Leo.

No wonder he was all smiles when he saw me at the party. I had just texted him that I accepted his apology for calling us the Fake Four!

But how did he get my number? And why wouldn't he identify himself?

Weird.

My hands are shaking when I go to change his contact name from *Locke* to *Leo*, rereading our last conversation and realizing he was the one who warned me Coach was looking for me. But before I hit SAVE, I stop. Charlie will have my phone tomorrow. He thinks Locke is the one who texted me earlier because that's who I thought it was. And the last thing I want to deal with is hearing how I shouldn't be fraternizing with the enemy, which will definitely happen if Charlie snoops through my phone or if Leo texts me while he has it. So I change the contact name to a capital *L*.

And now I think about how to respond in a way where I get my questions answered but don't look like an idiot.

ME: It's a deal. And also curious, how'd you get my number?

Okay, so not very subtle.

L: I've had it for years. Back from when Nonna did that big group text freshman year with those pics of us from when we were kids.

L: I'm just now realizing you didn't save my number back then like I saved yours

L: Feeling super cool right about now

There's a smile bursting across my face. Bursting.

ME: I probably did but I lost my phone last year and all my
contacts

L: Don't try to make me feel better!

ME: Okay then you're right I totally didn't save your number

L: Okay never mind I take it back you can lie to me

I laugh out loud and then want to pull the sheet over my
face because I'm embarrassed for myself.

ME: We're starting over. But these are the off limit topics: MJ,
JL, Evil Joes, Maggie Mae, Charlie, Sophie, Wes, Fab Four,
Fake Four and why I'm at the golf course. These terms are non
negotiable

Mainly, I'm trying to stop future Leo from saying something about Charlie to Charlie tomorrow.

L: Those words have been stricken from my vocabulary

As much as I hate it, I delete the messages that mention
any of the now-taboo names or give any hint that this is Leo
instead of Locke. I've just gotten our conversation all cleaned
up when a few more messages come in from him.

L: Don't forget sunblock this time

L: Hydrate too it's gonna be hot

ME: Thanks for all the tips. Good luck tomorrow!

Honestly, good luck to us both, because we're both going to need it.

Boots & Bling
honoring
Danlee

Wednesday, May 11th
11:00 am

Truth #6: If there is a party, Charlie
will always become its star

Wednesday, May 11th, Morning

Olivia

Charlie drags in at the last possible moment. I have no idea what time he and Sophie and Wes got home last night. I was out the second my head hit the pillow, despite being a little keyed up from the Uber ride home and the texts from Leo, but when I woke up this morning, Sophie was asleep in the bed next to me.

I wish she didn't have plans with her mom today, because Sophie handled my mom like a champ, even if she overdid it a bit. I looked back through the texts and Sophie made me sound *very happy!!* But Mom loved it and commented several times that she was glad I was having *such a great day!!*

But since today it's back to Charlie being me again, I feel sure we're going to get busted by lunch.

Charlie walked right in, handed me his phone, then crashed on the couch like last time. I set an alarm on mine before leaving it on the floor next to him to make sure he doesn't oversleep. Okay, so I actually set three alarms. Ten minutes apart. He's going to be thrilled.

Whatever cream Nonna gave Sophie last night worked wonders, since I'm a lighter shade of red and pain-free. I slathered a ton of sunblock on and plan to reapply every two hours.

Choosing my most upbeat playlist, I crank the music up so loud I can't think about any of the things that could go wrong today. I'm trying to get my mind right. It's going to be hot without a cloud in sight if my weather app is to be trusted. And from the schedule I found on the tournament website, it's also going to be a long day. I cast a glance at the bag in the passenger seat that has my western-themed outfit and boots. There's probably no chance I can leave, if yesterday's attempt is any indication. But I'm hopeful!

I've also got to figure out how to handle Leo. Will it be awkward if I run into him today? He's keeping a secret for me, but for how long? It doesn't help that he thinks we're mean to the Evil Joes, but he has NO IDEA what those girls have done to us over the years. Now that I think about it, I should be mad at him for forming opinions on things he doesn't understand.

And then there are the tournament rules. Lily gave me a booklet yesterday before I left the course, and oh my God there are so many rules. I tried really hard to read them all, but I didn't get through the whole booklet. And some of them don't even make sense! One was *Don't give advice.* Yeah, okay, no problem. I have no advice to give!

I'm not sure if I'm supposed to enforce the rules or tattle on the players, though. I'm hoping she was just trying to educate me.

But what I'm not expecting is the traffic to get into this place. I circle the lot twice before I find a spot to park.

From what I've gathered in my internet research and eavesdropping, some of these tournaments are for school teams and some are for individual players. This one is the individual player type, and it looks like every player has a parent or coach with them. There will be three days of play, the third day ending with an awards thingy.

As I walk up to the clubhouse, I can easily spot the tournament officials. They're all wearing matching shirts and hats with their logo embroidered on each one. Since Coach Cantu works for the club (and I work for him) our main function is to make sure there are no issues with the course and to support the tournament people in any way we can.

I find Coach and Lily next to the doors where the balls and pyramid molds are kept.

Of course Coach checks his watch before he says,

"Morning, Olivia. Just like yesterday, let's get each station ready." He hands me a walkie-talkie and I clip it to the waistband of my mom shorts.

Thankfully, Lily helps, and we move down the line much faster than I did yesterday, although I still have a hard time getting a pyramid exactly right.

"Is this everyone who's playing in the tournament?" I ask. While there are a lot of people here, only about half are players.

Lily finishes another perfect stack on her first try. "Players will trickle in all morning. There are different tee-off times based on how the player is ranked. The better you are, the later you start."

"Yeah, that makes sense." I mean, it doesn't at all, but I'm tired of looking stupid when it comes to golf. There's already a line ready to start practicing, so we quickly get the last few pyramids finished, knowing we'll have to start all over shortly.

After an hour of constantly replenishing balls, Coach Cantu calls for me over the walkie-talkie.

"Olivia, meet me at the check-in table," he says over the static.

"Yes, Coach," I answer, and walk across the green grass to a long table set up on the back patio of the clubhouse.

"Hey, Coach," I say when I come up next to him.

"Olivia, this is Donald Williams, one of the tournament officials. You're going to drive him around today."

Mr. Williams barely spares me a glance. "Nice to meet you, Olivia." His right arm is in a cast and sling and he's studying a clipboard in his left hand.

Coach turns toward me and leans in close, his voice dropping to a whisper. "Normally, they drive themselves around, but obviously he needs some help. Your only job is to take him where he wants to go. Remember what I said about staying still and quiet while someone is teeing off, and stay to the cart paths. Reach out if you need anything."

Coach leaves, and I'm left with Mr. Williams, who is still ignoring me. "I'll go get a cart and pick you up just over there," I say, pointing to an open area to the right of the patio.

As I walk to get the cart, I pull out Charlie's phone so I can text him.

ME: I have to drive this guy around all day so there's no way I'm making the party at 11. I need you to hang out near Danlee's house though. Sorry!! Text me if you need me and I'll get back to you as soon as possible

He's probably still sleeping; the alarms aren't set to go off for another thirty minutes.

I grab the closest cart and pull it around to pick up Mr. Williams. He's got a bag, a box, a clipboard, and a cooler bag, and it takes us a few minutes to get everything loaded just the way he likes. It takes about thirty seconds for me to realize he's very particular. Like ridiculously so.

The clipboard has a list of all the players and their start times and other information I can't decipher. A glance at the top sheet shows the lineup for the guys, with Leo starting in third place and Locke just a few spots behind him. Those are the only names I recognize before he moves the clipboard out of view.

I wish I'd paid more attention to what Coach was saying this past semester, because it's killing me not knowing what all these numbers and terms mean.

Mr. Williams seems to finally get settled. His clipboard in his lap, his phone in the cupholder, and a pen in his left hand. "Okay, let's start at the tee box for hole one. I want you to pull up to each hole and stop. I will tell you when and where I want to go next. Please do not speak to me or anyone unless I tell you it's okay."

I nod, afraid to even answer him, and put the cart in drive. It lurches forward, but at least he doesn't fly out of the open front window.

We don't have far to go, and I pull up just off the tee box. I sit still while he makes notes on his clipboard although it's obvious he's struggling with using his left hand to write. I think about offering to write for him, but he told me not to speak, so I keep quiet. After a few minutes, he seems satisfied.

"Tee box two." And since I don't move as quickly as he thinks I should, he adds a clipped "Now."

We watch players. He asks the spectators to be quiet or to move back to the cart path. He makes notes on his clipboard. He talks on the walkie-talkie. I see various players from my school on different holes. Locke's on seven, while Cal and David are on eight and nine. The girls from my school are on the back side of the course on holes eleven, fourteen, and sixteen. Since Locke was the first familiar face I saw, I gave a small wave when we made eye contact, but the grunt from Mr. Williams had me pulling my arm back down. Now I ignore everyone else I see, not wanting to get any of us in any trouble. I hope they know I'm trying to follow the rules.

The entire time, Charlie's phone is vibrating in my back pocket. I'm praying these are texts meant for him and not him trying to reach me.

We're starting back over at the tee box for hole one when I spot Leo.

There are four players who will tee off from this box once the golfers ahead of them clear out of the way. Leo is holding his club out in front of him and doing some side-to-side stretch. He hasn't seen me yet, so I take a little moment to stare at him.

He's wearing soft gray pants and a white-collared golf shirt that pops against his tan skin. His curls are out of control, twisting around the edge of his baseball cap. The cap itself is worn-looking and faded. You can tell it used to be dark blue but is now almost a soft purple. It makes me think it means something to him, since all of his other clothes look pressed and fresh.

I'm still eyeing him up and down, so it's embarrassing when I get back to his face and he's staring right at me. Smirk and all. I giggle, then turn away and collide with Mr. Williams's glare.

"So how many golfers do you know who are playing today?"

I do a quick count. "Seven," I respond quietly.

"Will this be a problem?" he asks.

I'm shaking my head. "No. No, sir. Not at all."

Mr. Williams puts his clipboard on the dash and gets out of the cart. He moves around to the front as if wanting a closer view of what's happening at box one.

I avoid looking at Leo again but do take the opportunity to check the phone, since it's still going nuts in my back pocket. Texts from Bianca. Lots of them. While Mr. Williams is watching the players tee off and trying to write on that clipboard, I open the messages. I mean, what if it's something important I need to tell Charlie about?

Except they aren't messages. They are pictures of her in her costume for today's western party. And she looks adorable.

BIANCA: Too much??? I may be the only one there in Daisy Dukes!

BIANCA: Would that be bad??

I can't leave her hanging like that. And I can't call Charlie with Mr. Williams right in front of me. I make an executive decision to answer like I know Charlie would.

CHARLIE: 🔥🔥🔥🔥🔥

Charlie is a man of few words. She sends back the blowing-kisses emoji and I know I made the right choice.

Finally, Mr. Williams returns and gets into the cart. "Okay, let's move to the next tee box."

It takes everything in me not to glance at Leo before driving away.

Phone Duty: Charlie

I eye Olivia's phone like it's possessed. That stupid alarm has gone off three times even though I pushed END and not SNOOZE. But I'm ready for Aunt Lisa this time. At the first text that comes through, I reply, Jumping in the shower. I know how long it takes Olivia and Sophie to get dressed, so that should buy me an hour at least. It sucks I'm awake now, though.

I open every cabinet checking for food. Nothing looks good. Next is the pantry. Score! Cocoa Puffs for the win. Then I move to the fridge, but all hope for a bowl of chocolaty goodness is ruined when I spy the organic almond milk.

Aunt Lisa really is a monster.

I put the cereal back, then check out what else is in the fridge. Turkey bacon. Nope. Fruit. Nope. Yogurt—some with fruit, some without. Nope, nope. There is no food here. Now I'm awake and hungry. I consider walking down to Nonna's for breakfast until I remember that fiasco yesterday when Aunt Lisa thought Olivia was there. Maybe I'll go to Wes's. They usually have food. I go to pick up Olivia's phone but remember I just told Aunt Lisa that Olivia was in the shower.

"Is there coffee?"

I scream, then Sophie screams because I screamed.

"Damn! I forgot you were here," I say.

"You have slammed every cabinet in this room. I could hear you upstairs." She moves to the counter and pulls out the stuff to make coffee.

I open the fridge once more. "There's no good food here."

"Nonna probably has breakfast," Sophie mumbles.

"Yeah, I know, but . . ." I jump up and grab Olivia's phone from the table, then slide it across the counter to Sophie. "Man the phone. I'll be right back!"

But she is so much faster than me. "Not my day! I have to

head home to meet Mom!" She abandons the coffee and flies out of the back door. I swear I can hear her cackling.

Desperate times call for desperate measures. I'm leaving the phone. Olivia is supposed to be in the shower anyway, so it's not like she would text back right now. Sliding into my flip-flops, I'm out the door quick enough to see Sophie's car hasn't even left the street yet.

I can smell the cinnamon rolls before I even open Nonna's back door. There are only a few family members here this morning. Uncle Sal and my cousin Banks. Aunt Kelsey, but she only has two of her four daughters with her, Mary and Frannie. And of course, Nonna and Papa.

"Man, that smells good," I say. Nonna hugs me tight because I'm her favorite.

"Wes didn't want breakfast? Or the girls?" she asks, looking around the kitchen to make sure they didn't sneak in without her seeing them.

"Nope. Just me!"

"I haven't seen Olivia in days," she says.

I shrug, then shove a whole cinnamon roll in my mouth so I can't answer any questions. She's looking at me funny. And I don't like it.

"This is a busy week for them, Mom," Aunt Kelsey says.

I wish I could high-five her!

"Well, Michael will get to town this afternoon, so family

dinner here tonight. I'll send out a text." Nonna picks up her phone and within a few minutes, everyone's phone dings with a notification.

I finish eating and clean my dishes. "Thanks, Nonna!" I say, then haul it back to Olivia's. Once I'm back in her kitchen, I approach her phone cautiously.

And sure enough, there it is below Nonna's message.

MOM: What top are you wearing with the denim skirt? Something red would be cute! Maybe that tank we got in Dallas? You'll need a strapless bra with it though.

I stand next to the table, my hands on my hips. What the hell. Here we go again. Knowing I can't call Olivia unless it's an emergency—although this is like an emergency!—I call Sophie instead.

"Hey," Sophie says when she answers. "Trouble already? I just left like twenty minutes ago."

"On your day, did Aunt Lisa talk about what bra Olivia should wear, or is it just me? Because I think it's just me. Like a curse."

"Haha, I wish I could see your face!"

She's amused by this. Typical.

I read Aunt Lisa's text to her.

"You can just answer *Okay* to that."

"Is it weird she takes this much interest in Olivia?" I ask.

"A little. I think she's freaking out that Olivia is leaving soon."

"But your mom isn't acting like this. Or is she? Don't tell me Aunt Eileen is a weirdo, too. I don't think I can take it." I type in the response Sophie suggested and pray there's no follow-up.

"Mom has Margot and Anna. I mean, I think she's sad I'm leaving, but honestly, I'll be in south Louisiana, close to Margot, she's probably thinking it works out better, since she'll get to visit Anna more."

Those three dots are jumping around. "Stay on with me. Another text incoming."

MOM: That denim skirt is a little short. You may want to wear some boy shorts just to be on the safe side.

"And now we're talking about underwear." I read Sophie the latest text.

Sophie loses it. She's actually snorting, she's laughing so hard. If I didn't need her right now, I'd hang up on her.

"Again, a simple *Okay* should be enough," she finally manages to say.

"It's only nine thirty in the morning. How am I supposed to do this all day?"

"You'll survive! Gotta go, Wes is calling." Then she ends the call.

Oh, great. Another text. What else could Aunt Lisa want? I'm about to get Sophie back on the phone, but I see it's not from Aunt Lisa. The contact name is *L*.

L? I open the message.

L: Looks like you got a pretty cush job today

I scroll up and read the couple of texts from last night. Well, well, well, seems like Olivia and Locke have hit it off. I guess she doesn't know Sophie told me who was sending these texts yesterday if she's trying to hide him behind the first letter of his name. That's cute.

I'm totally going to respond.

ME: Yeah it's pretty sweet

It doesn't take long before he's typing back. I let out an evil laugh. This is pretty fun.

L: Are you stuck with that guy all day?

Oh. Wait. This may be trickier than I thought it would be. It takes me a second, but I reply:

ME: Not sure yet

L: Maybe I'll see you when he's not around

She's probably going to kill me for this.

ME: Come find me later

Today may not be as bad as I thought it would be.

Olivia

I get thirty glorious minutes for lunch. But mostly thirty glorious minutes away from Mr. Williams. If there was a machine that could suck the fun out of every little thing around you, it would be modeled after him. I tried to say hi to Tanika when she was waiting to tee off and was only three feet away and literally doing nothing, but Mr. Williams popped my arm with his clipboard and said, "No talking to the players."

If I didn't need this to graduate, I would have popped him right back in his bad arm.

But for now, I'm eating a box lunch while hiding behind a tree near the back patio of the clubhouse. Mr. Williams is in the dining room and all the players are on the course, so this area is pretty deserted.

I call Charlie, since by now he should be sitting outside the party in his car.

He answers on the third ring. "Hey!"

The background noise on the call is loud. "What's going on? I hope you're parked in front of Danlee's house!"

"Yeah! That's it! That's where I am!"

"Why is it so loud?" I ask. I put my box lunch down on the grass and start to pace. He'd better not be screwing this up.

"It's the radio," he says.

He's lying.

"Charlie—" I start, but he interrupts me.

"I'll call you back." And then he ends the call.

Crap! I'm going to kill him.

"You made it tough to find you," I hear a voice behind me say. I spin around and there's Leo.

A flare of giddiness rushes through me at the thought that he was looking for me. I keep my smile in check. Small, to show I'm happy to see him, but not so big I give away more than I want.

He's still somehow fresh and clean, while I'm sure I look a hot mess. My hair has been blown in every direction from being in that golf cart with no windshield. And it's hot. Really hot. There's a good chance I stink.

He nods to where my box is sitting on the ground. "Lunch break?"

"Oh yeah. Thirty whole minutes!"

He moves closer to me and I resist doing a quick smell check under my arms.

"Are you on a lunch break, too?"

"No, just finished the first nine holes. We're moving faster than the group in front of us, so I have a few minutes to get something to drink," he says, shaking the white Styrofoam cup in his hand with the club's logo on it.

"So how is it going today?" I ask him.

He shrugs. "Hanging in there. This is a tough course and so we're all struggling a little. It's fine, though, if we're all off our game. How's your day going?"

I roll my eyes. "I'm driving the hall monitor around. Not only is he making sure no one is doing anything wrong, he's hoping they have the most miserable time in the process."

"Yeah, that guy sucks. I've done tournaments with him before and there is no gray area with him. At all."

"I hope this isn't what I'm doing every day. Although it's better than stacking those balls into pyramids. Whoever came up with that idea is dead to me."

He laughs and I really like the sound of it. He's even cuter when that big grin breaks across his face.

"A lot of courses I've played at just hand you a bucket of balls. I thought you were here working with the tournament people, but I guess you're with the club if they've got you putting out range balls."

I put my hands on my hips. "Is this your less-than-subtle

way of asking me why I'm here? Our first conversation and you're already breaking the rules."

He can tell I'm not too serious. Leo holds both hands out in front of him, cup and all. "No, not our first. I actually waited until the second conversation today. And no, I'm not breaking any rules. I'm not asking why. It's more of a what. I thought since you were driving Williams around, you were here with the tournament."

The first part of his sentence catches me off guard. And clues me in to the chance that he texted me and Charlie responded. I'm thankful I didn't put his real name in my phone but terrified about what that conversation entailed.

Although he came looking for me, so it can't be too bad.

"I'm sure you saw Mr. Williams has his arm in a sling. I'm his chauffeur." I do a bow/curtsy thing that really doesn't make sense.

The heat is definitely getting to me, but thankfully he's still grinning.

Leo glances toward the course and then back to me. "I've gotta get back out there." But something about his tone and posture makes me think he's not ready to leave, and that makes me happy.

"I'm sure I'll see you when we make our rounds. But I'm not allowed to talk to you, so just know I'm not ignoring you on purpose."

That smile. Was it always this cute? Or maybe I'm just

noticing it now because back then it would have never been directed at me.

"I know. Lots of rules at these things." And then he's gone. I drop back down on the ground so I can finish my lunch. I think about asking Charlie if he's texting "L," but all that would do is make sure he does. With my social life in his hands, I just have to hope it's not as bad as it could be.

Phone Duty: Charlie

"I should have made Wes come with me," I say out loud. To no one. Since I'm in the car by myself.

A couple of girls I know walk up the long driveway toward Danlee's house and I sink a little farther in my seat. I feel like such a creeper. Danlee lives right outside of town on a big chunk of land and there's nowhere to hide.

When I first looked at the invitation, I knew the party was at Danlee's house but didn't think much about it until Aunt Lisa texted, Don't be late, you know how far out she lives. I left early so "Olivia" would arrive on time, because no, I had no idea how far out she lived. But apparently no one arrives on time, since I was the first one here?

I've watched each girl arrive . . . in costume . . . and that's been interesting. There's no way that belt buckle Steph is wearing isn't dragging her down. No way.

But I'm also freaking out that someone is going to see me, because I look like a perv creeper sitting on the side of the driveway like this.

Tap, tap, tap.

"Shit!" I yell, and jump in my seat.

Bianca is laughing at me while I roll my window down.

"Charlie, I didn't mean to scare you."

She can barely contain herself.

"What are you doing here?" I'm sure she's wondering why I'm sitting in the car in front of Danlee's house by myself.

I don't want to out Olivia, so I'm left with looking like an idiot.

"I was waiting for Olivia. She left her bag in my truck and I knew she'd be here." Dumbest lie ever.

"Oh," she says.

And then I get a better look at her. She looks good. Really, really good. Opening the truck door, I hop out. "I'm liking this outfit."

"Better in person, huh," she says, then twirls around and does this cute little heel kick thing in those cowboy boots.

"Uh, yeah," I say, not really following.

Bianca and I have been flirting all week. I like her. A lot. But I'm nervous about starting something with her, since we'll be going our separate ways come fall. So as long as we're both cool with keeping things easy, I'm all game.

Another few cars pull up and she glances at the road, probably looking for Olivia's car. "We haven't seen much of Olivia this week. Kind of weird, actually. Want me to take her bag in with me?"

"No, I'll give her a few more minutes. I think she needed something in it before going into the party."

And now *that's* the dumbest lie ever. I'm digging a hole and I'll be buried alive under all these lies.

"Okay, I'll see you later, then," she says, taking a few steps away from me. "Won't I?"

I close the gap she just made between us. "That can be arranged. I have family dinner tonight, but Judd's band is playing at Superior after. Want to meet up there?"

"Judd's in a band?" I haven't found a person who wasn't shocked by this development.

"Yeah, come watch them with me."

She smiles, then tucks a piece of hair behind her ear while biting her bottom lip. I don't care if she's practiced that a thousand times in the mirror, because it's worth it.

"I'll meet you there."

She walks up the driveway and gives me a wave before disappearing inside. Yee. Haw.

A few more cars arrive and park down the street. I recognize the Evil Joes' car and let out a moan. This is the last thing I need.

I slide down low in my seat again. I know they'll recognize my truck, but maybe they won't see me. Of course they're dressed identically in matching dresses and cowboy boots. And they did something weird with their hair. It's in some complicated braid thing that sort of makes them look like they have horns.

Or maybe their real horns are starting to show and they're just trying to cover them up.

They stroll past my truck and start whispering. Then they stop.

Great. This is friggin' great.

They stand in front of my truck and Mary Jo beats her hands on my hood.

I shoot up in my seat, giving myself away before I can even think twice about it.

"Hey!" I yell through my closed window.

"Weirdo," Jo Lynn says.

Mary Jo adds, "Why are you here?"

I roll down my window. There are so many things I want to say, but I stop myself. I will not let them screw with me.

I wave them off and they finally walk away. The phone buzzes; it's Aunt Lisa again. This day cannot end soon enough.

Surely she sees Olivia is here.

MOM: Take pics of the flowers and food. Dad and I are throwing a party for the Fletchers next month and I'm thinking about using the same florist but want to see how everything looks. Same with the caterer.

MOM: And I heard there will be a line dance! Would love a video of that!!

MOM: Have fun! You know I'd love a picture of you and your friends but I'm not holding my breath!

What the . . . Are you freaking kidding me? Pictures of the flowers? And food? Sure, no problem, I'll just multiply my creeper level by ten.

I know Bailey is inside the party already, so I pull up a text to her. God, I hope this works.

ME: Hey! I'm not going to make it. Please tell Danlee I'm so sorry I got caught up at work again. But mom is driving me nuts about getting pics of the food and flowers. Will you take some and send them to me please??

I read it a few times before I hit SEND. If she calls me back instead of texting, I'm screwed. Thankfully, her response comes pretty quick.

BAILEY: No prob I'll send them

Then there's another one.

BAILEY: I didn't think you were working today

I lean back and rub a hand across my face, giving myself a second to think.

ME: Nonna was shorthanded. I couldn't tell her no

After a couple minutes, Olivia's phone starts vibrating and *yes*, Bailey is coming through with the pics. I save them to Olivia's camera roll, then turn right around and send them to Aunt Lisa.

I'm debating how long I need to stay here to satisfy Aunt Lisa. Or maybe I can dump Olivia's phone in the mailbox and come back for it. But what if the mail hasn't been delivered yet today and the carrier accidentally takes it? Yeah, that would be bad.

Bianca catches my attention as I'm thinking about all my options. She's walking back down the driveway toward my truck, her legs looking particularly long in those short shorts. Man, I love a themed party.

I roll down the window again and try to think about what I'll say when she asks why I'm still here.

Bianca leans against my door, half hanging in the window.

"Bailey just sent Olivia a bunch of pics of the flowers and food because she's not coming. Stuck at work. Did she not tell you?"

I let out a nervous laugh and pick up Olivia's phone, trying to hide the floral case. "She just called."

Bianca gives me a grin. "Okay, well, I wanted to make sure you weren't still waiting for her. I tried to text, but you didn't respond."

Uh-oh. I hold the phone up in the air again and move it around. "Reception sucks out here."

She steps away from my truck and slowly walks back to the house. But of course I'm not leaving and she's curious why. Just before she gets to the door, she comes back and I roll the window back down. Again.

"Are you creeping around here for anyone in particular?"

If I could bang my head against the steering wheel I would. "No. I . . . it's complicated." The last thing Olivia would want anyone to know is that she's on the verge of not graduating. School has been her thing since we were little, and I know how hard she worked to get to the top of our class. I want so badly to be mad at Olivia about this, but no matter what I wanted to do and no matter how stupid the idea was, she was always right there with me. I mean, she was usually outlining why it was a dumb idea and how quickly we would get caught, but she was still there. I guess I'm going to look like a dumbass for sitting out here.

Bianca tilts her head toward the house. "Danlee's mom got this old guy who plays a fiddle. He's just about to start. Come see?"

"No. I'm good."

But she's opening my door and pulling me out. "Seriously, come on. I heard he's amazing."

This is a bad idea. It's clearly a girl party, and the Evil Joes are in there, but Bianca isn't taking no for an answer.

"I'll go in, but we're staying in the back," I say.

We weave our way through Danlee's house to the doors leading to the backyard. A stone path goes down a small hill to a barn and corral area with several horses in the pasture, but it's the inside of the barn that blows me away. There are lights strung across the ceiling in a crisscross pattern and hay bales topped with a piece of burlap for people to sit on. Big metal troughs are filled with ice and drinks and there's a long table full of barbecue.

Bianca keeps going, but I dig my heels in. "I'm staying back here or I'm going back to my truck."

She lets out a huff but gives in. We find two hay bales away from the crowd. Luckily, everyone's attention is on the old guy on the other side of the barn.

He picks up his fiddle and plucks a couple strings. Then he just goes to town on it. I mean, I'm surprised there's no smoke rising from his bow. Once he finishes the first song, he invites the girls up for some line dancing. I take this opportunity to film a few seconds of it so I can get Aunt Lisa off my back. Then I snag some ribs because holy cow they smell delicious. After a couple of songs—and a full plate of food—I feel like I've stayed long enough, but the old guy starts talking.

"Okay, now it's time for the real fun! Y'all ready to turn this hoedown into a rodeo?"

He pulls on a rope and what I thought was just the backdrop to his show was really a curtain hiding a massive mechanical bull.

"Who's ready for their eight seconds?" he yells.

A few groups of girls start giggling and threaten to push each other over there, but no one takes him up on his offer.

And then I feel my arm lifting.

Bianca is holding it up high while waving hers around. "Charlie wants to try!"

What! Charlie does not!

The old dude gestures for me to come forward.

"What'd you do?" I ask her.

Her shoulders draw up to her ears and she gives me a funny look. "No one was volunteering! It felt awkward!"

She pushes me over to where the man is waiting for me while the rest of the girls are clapping and cheering my name.

"I'm going to die," I say.

"Don't be so dramatic!" she replies.

Once I'm close enough, he pulls me next to him. "From the chants, I'm guessing you're Charlie!" he says.

"Yep." Maybe I shouldn't have had that second scoop of potato salad. The Evil Joes look positively giddy that I'm up here; their phones are ready to record the carnage.

He hands me a glove and asks, "Need a boost?"

This is already going to be humiliating. I don't need to add to it, so that's a firm no. I heave one leg over and try to hop up on the giant thing.

As much as I was hoping I could make it on my first try, I do not. Not my second either.

Third time is a charm!

The old man signals to a guy sitting off to the side behind a control board and the bull pitches forward. I clutch the reins with my gloved hand and hold on for dear life. It starts out slow, moving back and forth in a circle just long enough to relax. Then it really gets going.

My knees are locked in tight and I've got my free hand up in the air.

And I'm still on!

I am amazing at this!

The girls are on their feet, cheering for me, but they're all a blur as I spin by them.

This is awesome!

The bull starts slowing down, and instead of jumping off, I stand up on it, raising both fists in the air *Rocky*-style, and scream, "Wooooo-hoooooo!"

And the crowd goes wild.

When the bull finally stops, I leap off. More cheers.

"Very good, Charlie!" the old man says.

"That was the coolest thing ever!"

I'm walking back to Bianca, high-fiving everyone I pass, when I feel Olivia's phone start vibrating in my back pocket. I pull it out and see my name on the screen.

"Hey!" I say.

"What is that noise? I hope you're parked in front of Danlee's house!"

I have to hold one hand against my opposite ear just to hear her. The cheers are so loud. "Yeah! That's it! That's where I am!"

"Why is it so loud?" she asks.

I step a few feet away. "It's the radio." She's going to know I'm lying.

"Charlie—" she starts, but I interrupt her.

"I'll call you back," I scream into the phone, and then end the call, finally making my way to Bianca.

She throws her arms around me. "You were incredible!"

I lift her off the ground, giving her a little twirl. "That was the coolest thing I've ever done." I set her down, one hand on her waist and the other linked with hers. "I'm going to slip out now. Thanks for dragging me in. That was really fun."

She leans forward. We're close. And I like it. "See you later, Charlie Messina."

And I like how she uses my whole name, and she knows it.

She starts to move away and I hang on to her hand until the last possible second.

Once I'm back in the truck, the phone vibrates again.

MOM: Don't forget to send me a video of the line dancing!

I send her the video I took. And then I get another text. I cackle when I see who it's from. Good ole letter *L*.

L: Done for today. Is there a party tonight? Wouldn't mind running into you again

Oh, this guy is smooth. I prop Olivia's phone against the steering wheel and rub my hands together, thinking of the perfect response. There isn't a party tonight, and I know we have to eat family dinner at Nonna's, but then there's Judd's thing at Superior. Perfect.

ME: No parties tonight ☹ And I have to eat family dinner at my grandmother's house but then I'll be at Superior watching a friend's band play. It would be easy to run into me there

It doesn't take him long to text back.

L: I'm sure I'll have dinner plans too but will also feel like going to watch a band after. It will be purely a coincidence

Ha! I like this guy! And then I delete the last three messages but leave the one from earlier. Olivia would kill me if she knew I was setting up a meeting between her and Locke. And then she'd back out of going to watch Judd play. Can't have that.

It's been all about school and grades and graduation and nothing else with Olivia lately. She'd be happy to flirt with Locke for weeks without ever pulling the trigger on meeting up with him. She just needs a little push.

After dinner at Nonna's, we'll go to Superior. And what? Surprise, look who's here.

She'll thank me later.

TONIGHT ONLY!

WILDER BLUE

Superior Grill
7 PM

Truth #7: Drum solos are a full-contact sport

Wednesday, May 11th, Afternoon

Olivia

While day two wasn't as strenuous as day one, it was still a long day. Especially spending as many hours as I did in Mr. Williams's presence. I'm not sure which was the most oppressive, him or the heat. I saw Leo a few times during the day but never had a chance to talk to him again, and I'm surprised by how bummed out that makes me.

I'm dying to retrieve my phone from Charlie. He's got some explaining to do.

Almost every social media post shows him riding a mechanical bull and screaming *Yeehaw!* I mean, it's everywhere! So much for him staying in the car in front of Danlee's house.

But I'm also dying to see if Leo texted me. If Charlie had figured out L was Leo instead of Locke, I definitely would have heard about it by now.

Nonna sent out a text to everyone this morning about family dinner, since Uncle Michael is in town, and then Wes reminded us about Judd's musical debut at Superior, and I could cry just thinking about how long it'll be before I get to go to bed.

Family dinner. Don't know if I have the energy for that. But Leo will probably be at dinner, too, since he's staying with the Evil Joes, and that makes me feel . . . excited? Nervous? A little of both?

But then, the Evil Joes will be there, and Charlie, Sophie, and Wes, and I'm back to wanting to crawl into bed until tomorrow. How did everything get *more* complicated?

Charlie is waiting for me at my house when I pull up. He's on the front porch and meets me at my car the second I put it in park.

"Take it. I'm done. Out. Off the clock." He's shoving my phone in my hand before I'm even out of the car. "I love Aunt Lisa, I really do, but I need to be done for the day."

I roll my eyes, trading phones with him. "Lightweight."

His shrugs, shaking his head. "I'll take it. I'm a lightweight. You're the queen."

"Looks like you put on quite the show at the party," I say.

He's beaming. "That was insane! Did you see it?" He's bouncing up and down, he's so excited.

I punch him in the arm. "Of course I did! Everyone did! Your phone has been blowing up all afternoon."

He swipes it open and starts checking his messages as he walks away. His laugh floats down the street as he reads them all, and I'm afraid his head is going to be too big to make it through Nonna's back door by dinnertime. "Bianca definitely looked five-flame-emojis hot! Good call!" he calls over his shoulder. "Heading to Wes's, then going to Nonna's. Don't forget about family dinner!"

"Apparently, you're the one who needs reminding! The other half of your texts today were from every family member telling you not to forget about tonight," I yell back.

All he does is wave his hand in the air and keep walking.

Dragging myself inside, I collapse on the couch in the den. I may never leave this spot.

My phone vibrates. It's Mom. She's actually calling instead of texting and I'm thankful I got here when I did.

"Hey," I say when I answer.

"You sound tired," she says.

If she only knew. "Not too bad. How's it going down there?"

"Oh, fine. Just a lot of long days staring at numbers. Hoping to wrap it up Friday morning and head back."

I'm glad she can't see my expression because . . . *Friday*

morning?! If she leaves too early, I may not be done at the course before she pulls into town.

"That's great," I say, with as much enthusiasm as I can muster.

She talks and talks and I reply when an "Uh-huh" isn't enough.

"Well, I'm about to jump in the shower and then head to Nonna's," I say.

"I heard Michael has brought a special someone to town! Can't wait to hear what everyone thinks about him!"

Poor Uncle Michael's boyfriend. He has no idea what he's getting into.

Once I finally get off the call with Mom, I check my phone for texts I missed today, of course starting with Leo.

There are a couple of texts back and forth before Leo came and found me during my lunch break, but nothing new since then, and that's more disappointing than I thought it would be. Ignoring the rest, I head up to my room for a shower. Within thirty minutes, I'm on the way to Nonna's, and by the line of cars down the street, most everyone is already here. My mom should be the only sibling missing tonight, and Jake, Graham, and Margot should be the only cousins not here.

Chaos is the only word to describe my grandparents' house on family dinner night. And Nonna loves every minute of it.

I sneak in the back door . . . or at least I think I sneak in, but I hear a chorus of greetings the second I'm inside.

Nonna makes a beeline to me, squeezing me tight in a big hug. "I haven't seen you in forever."

So dramatic.

"I saw you on Sunday night," I answer as I hug her back. "And I was here the other day, but you were out. We had pizza!"

"Yes, I know, I heard all about it. We usually don't go so long between visits, though. I missed you."

She's laying it on thick. Sophie clued me in that Nonna knows something is going on, so I'm not surprised by the attention right now. Nonna's a bloodhound when it comes to sniffing out the truth in this family.

"It's a crazy week! So many parties." And then I pry myself away from her by saying, "Oh! There's Uncle Michael!"

Uncle Michael is the only one of Mom's siblings who hasn't gotten married yet, and in my family that is A BIG DEAL, all caps. Nonna lets me go and I head straight toward him. I am really happy to see him, since he hasn't been to town in forever. He throws open his arms when he spots me heading his way. I don't play favorites with family members, but if I did . . . Wait, I take that back. Who am I kidding? Of course I play favorites. And he's one of my top picks.

"Olivia!" he says as he wraps me in a hug. "I was about to walk down to your house and drag you back here."

I take a minute or so longer than necessary holding him close. "I'm glad you're here." My voice breaks on the last word.

He pulls back and looks at me, concern on his face. And I'm shocked by the water gathering in my eyes.

"Everything okay?" he whispers. "Want to go find a spot to talk?"

I shake my head. "No, I'm good. Just happy to see you." I can tell he knows there's more, but he doesn't push. It's one of the reasons I love him. Whenever he's in town, we go to movies or grab dinner or hang out here at Nonna's. He's more like a big brother than an uncle to me.

He pulls me to the side, keeping his arm around me. "Olivia, I want you to meet Tim. Tim, this is my niece, Olivia."

I can tell by Uncle Michael's face that Tim is someone special. I like him immediately.

"He's told me all about you! Salutatorian! Congrats," Tim cheers. And now I could really cry.

Uncle Michael and Tim are getting pulled away by Aunt Ayin to meet my cousin Sara, but Uncle Michael squeezes my hand before he goes and says, "Come find me later so we can talk."

I give him a small smile and he's gone.

Okay. Time to snap out of it. This is not the place to get emotional. Nonna can sniff that out like a shark with blood in the water. And no matter what, I can't tell Uncle Michael what's going on, because as much as I don't want to disappoint Mom and Dad, I don't want to disappoint him either.

Nonna yells above the chatter, "Everyone make a plate and find a seat!"

I let the crowd thin out before moving down the buffet Nonna has set out on the counter. My hands full with my plate and a bottle of water, I spy Charlie, Wes, and Sophie across the room at one of the folding tables that gets dragged out when everyone is here.

Charlie is waving me over. "Hurry up. We need to fill this table before the Evil Joes get here," he says, then calls out to his sister, Sara, and our cousins Banks and Hannah.

Finally, every seat is taken and Charlie lets out a sigh of relief just as the Evil Joes march in through the back door. They are always late and Sophie swears they just like making an entrance.

Leo is right behind them.

Wes leans to the left so he can see past Sophie. "He's still in town?"

Sophie turns around. "Well, I guess so. There he is."

Wes throws his roll at her and she throws it right back, hitting him square in the forehead.

I act like Leo and I haven't been texting, and like we don't talk every chance we get when we're at the golf course. I act like I don't know exactly where he is at any given moment in this crowded room.

Leo and the Evil Joes end up at one of the tables on the

other side of the room, but he's sitting directly in my line of vision.

It is unsettling!

And when we do make eye contact, I think he's trying to hide as much as I am.

He'd get as much pushback from the Joes as I would from my side, and he knows it. They didn't want to share him with us back then, so there's no way they want to share him with us now.

My phone on the table vibrates with a text. Charlie's eyes go straight to it and I'm thankful it's facedown.

I slide it toward me, not turning it over until it's in my lap.

"Who's that?" he asks.

If the heat coming off them is any indication, my cheeks are in full bloom when I see the letter *L* on the screen.

"Bailey," I say.

He gives me an "Uh-huh" like he doesn't believe me.

I swipe open the message, making sure no one else can read it.

L: Hey! What's up? I'm eating dinner with my host family and they are much louder than I remember

I can't stop the laugh that pops out.

"I don't remember Bailey being that funny," Charlie says. He's got his eagle eye on me, watching my every move.

"She's hilarious," I say. Then I text Leo back.

ME: How strange! I'm eating with my family and they are also very loud!

Since Charlie is watching me, I don't look up at Leo but instead watch those three dots move and wait for his next text.

L: We have so much in common it's unreal
ME: How did you finish today? I thought I would see you but you were gone when I made the final round with Williams.
L: Holding my same place but I need to improve tomorrow
ME: I feel like you can do it!

I can't help it. I find him across the room and he's looking my way, too. Charlie is still watching me, but from where he's sitting, Leo is blocked by Uncle Sal and Uncle Marcus.

"It looks like Uncle Michael is really happy," Sophie says. "Hopefully we won't scare Tim off."

"Nonna would drag him back by his ear if he tries to run away," Charlie says.

Wes checks his watch. "We need to leave in about thirty minutes to catch the opening of Judd's band."

I chuckle. "Judd's band. I can't believe that's even a thing."

Hannah leans closer. She's Uncle Sal's oldest daughter

and just graduated from college last year. "Where are y'all going? To listen to a band?"

"Yeah, you want to come?" Wes asks. "The more people we bring, the better."

"Sure, I'm in. I'll see if Uncle Michael and Tim want to come, too. They may need a breather from Nonna."

She gets up with her empty plate and takes it to the sink before heading to the table across the room. Uncle Michael and Tim are sitting with the Evil Joes and I can tell the moment Charlie realizes what's about to happen.

"No. No. No. No, Hannah, no," he whispers. And sure enough, she has the entire table's attention. And they're all nodding along. Hannah turns back to Wes and calls from across the room, "They're all in!"

It's like a caravan from Nonna's to Superior. Even a few of my other uncles and aunts are joining us. Judd is going to be thrilled.

It takes a few laps around the parking lot before we can find a spot, and I'm wondering if this crowd knows what's in store. I mean, I'm not saying Judd can't play the drums, but I've known him a long time and I've never even seen him beat a pencil against his desk with any kind of rhythm.

Our group walks in and Judd jumps up and yells "Messina

family! Yes!" He gestures us to a table he reserved for us on the patio near the stage, but it's clear there aren't enough chairs. He should have known better.

Charlie and Wes help him drag more over, and now there are about twelve chairs around a table built for six. It's tight.

And of course, Leo ends up right across from me. Except this time, there's only about five feet separating us. I bet if I slid my foot forward, it would run right into his.

Charlie pulls up one more chair and boxes me in with it.

"Who's this for?" I ask, since everyone has a seat. "Bianca?"

He has a weird expression, then jumps up and drags an additional chair to the table, so now there's two of them. "I don't know. In case extras show up."

A waitress quickly puts chips and salsa on the table and takes our order. Since we just ate, we stick to drinks, with those who are old enough getting the margaritas this restaurant is famous for.

Bianca shows up just as the first round is served and slides into the chair right next to Charlie. She eyes the empty chair and starts to push it away so she has a little more room, but he stops her.

"We may need it," he shouts over the band's warm-up.

The band is ready to start, and Judd beats his drumsticks together, counting them down to the opening of their first song. He looks very professional and we are all duly impressed.

The band is . . . not good. But they aren't horrible either.

Given a few more weeks of practice, they could actually be decent. I feel sure one of the other members of the band must have a relative who owns this place and that's how they got the gig.

But Charlie and Wes cheer for them like it's the Jonas Brothers up there, loud squeals and all.

"How'd they get the name Wilder Blue?" Hannah asks.

Charlie rolls his eyes. "The lead singer lives in a blue house on Wilder. They practice in the garage."

After the first couple of songs, they seem to settle down a bit and it's a little better. Or we've gotten used to them.

Charlie keeps checking out the door where we came in. Enough so that it's obvious.

"Who are you waiting for?" I ask.

He shakes me off, but his gaze keeps bouncing from the stage to the door and back again.

"I'm going to the bathroom," I say to no one in particular, and head to a back hall in the main restaurant. There's a line, but it moves pretty fast. When I come out of the ladies' room, Leo is right there. I do a quick check but don't recognize anyone around him.

"Don't worry, no one on the off-limits list is nearby," he says. It was so loud on the patio that it seems weird to be able to hear him so clearly right now.

I move away from the line, farther down the hall, and he follows right behind me.

"I was looking forward to running into you here. But I was hoping for a little less of a crowd." His grin is a little lopsided and my heart goes to fluttering. I'm leaning against the wall and he's close. Close enough that I can see little specks of gold in those brown eyes.

"Yeah, it seems I'm always surrounded by family." Is my voice breathless? Oh God, I think it is.

"That's the main thing I remember about you. Always with . . . Look at me about to go off-limits." He jokes and I swear he's an inch closer.

A loud group of women turns the corner, headed for the bathroom, and we both jump. Leo's hand grips the back of his neck and he looks a little frustrated. Then that one eyebrow rises, so of course I have to match it.

The look he gives me is worth the risk of being discovered by my family.

I'm still staring into his eyes when his hand slides into mine and he pulls me down the hall and out the side door. It's dark and quiet out here. Judd's band is muffled and it makes them sound better than they are. And once again, my back is to the wall and he's standing in front of me. But this time not as close as I'd like.

"Look," I say, blowing out a long breath and a ton of my own frustration. "I know you probably think it's dumb that I want to . . . not hide this . . . that's not what I'm trying to do. I mean, whatever this is . . . and I'm not saying it's anything . . .

it's just so much easier if . . . you know who . . . we keep them out of it. I mean, you know what I mean."

He's laughing. Hard. I hang my head because I'm embarrassed by the flood of nonsense that just poured out of my mouth.

But then he's there. Arms around me, the top of my head resting against his chest. And he's talking quietly in my ear.

"I've never been around you without *them*. Any of them. Except for this week. And I like it. I like that I don't have to share you right now. I like that this is just ours and not theirs, too. Whatever this is. It doesn't have to be anything. Or it can be something."

My hands come up and I grab on to his biceps, making sure he doesn't step away too soon. Because I like this. A lot. But I'm also still a little embarrassed and it's easier to have him this close and not have to look at him.

"Okay," I mumble. I want to say more, but then I also want to keep everything I'm feeling to myself.

"Do you have to stay? Or could we leave?"

I finally pull back and meet his gaze. "Where would we go?"

He checks his watch. "I have about an hour before I need to get some sleep so I'm ready for tomorrow. And if I have a choice, I'd rather spend that hour somewhere a little quieter talking to you than in there listening to that band with half your family."

I'm chewing on my bottom lip, trying to figure out how we can both leave here without anyone knowing.

And as if he can read my mind, he says, "I already told the girls I was leaving. They know I wouldn't stay here long since I have to play tomorrow. You could go make an appearance at the table while I wait out here for an Uber. I'll text you when it gets here."

When I think about what I would like to do for the next hour, hanging out with Leo sounds like a pretty good choice.

"I drove, so I'll meet you at my car. Give me five minutes." I don't stay long enough to hear his answer or change my mind.

Judd's band is taking a break and Judd is sitting in the extra chair Charlie pulled up earlier.

"I don't know him and I'm not texting him," Judd says to Charlie as I walk up to the table.

"I can't believe he's not here," Charlie says, then jumps when he sees me. "Oh, hey!" And then he looks at the door again. I'm clearly missing something, but with Charlie, I don't even try to figure it out.

"Y'all sound so good!" I say to Judd. "I had no idea you could play the drums."

He wiggles his eyebrows. "Just wait until the next set. I have a solo."

"You're singing?" Sophie yells.

Judd holds up his drumsticks. "No. A drum solo."

"Oh, that's good," she says, and relaxes back in her seat.

I lean forward so Wes and Sophie can hear me, too. "I'm heading out. I'm so tired and have to do it all again tomorrow."

Wes is shaking his head. "This is the second night in a row you're bailing on us."

I shrug. "Sorry. Can't do it."

Charlie looks really torn. "Are you sure?"

"I'm positive. Can y'all catch a ride?"

"Yeah, for sure," Sophie answers.

Uncle Michael gets up from his seat and comes around the table. "Are you leaving?"

"Yes, I'm tired. Heading home."

He puts an arm around me and pulls me close. "Are you sure you're okay?"

I give him a big hug. "I swear. All good." And then I get out of here before he offers to ride home with me.

"Text me that you made it home!" Sophie yells as I walk away from the table.

Leo is leaning against my car when I make it to the parking lot. "I thought for a second you'd changed your mind."

"You know how hard it is to break away from that group. Lots of good-byes."

I unlock my car and we slide inside. "So where to?" I could offer for us to go back to my house since no one's there, but that seems a little more than what we are right now.

"Ice cream?" he asks.

"Oh, that sounds good."

There's a Baskin-Robbins not far from here. They have bright pink metal picnic tables out front and my absolute favorite flavor—peanut butter and chocolate.

Once we're inside and it's our turn to order, Leo has to try three or four samples before deciding what he wants. And he doesn't even pick one of the flavors he taste-tested.

"Weirdo," I say, and I swear the girl behind the counter wants to agree with me.

After a short back-and-forth between us, he pays for the ice cream after he reminds me I paid for the Uber last night so it's only fair.

Luckily there's an empty picnic table, and we sit across from each other.

"I'm guessing you're the kind who thinks he's going to get something different but always ends up with the same flavor every time," I tease.

He's smirking. It's cute. "I definitely like trying new things," he says. And then adds, "But I also like coming back to one I know is a favorite. Makes me appreciate it more."

And I'm not 100 percent sure we're still talking about ice cream.

"You're in Baton Rouge now?" I need to steer us to a safer subject.

"Actually, St. Francisville."

"Do you like it?"

A big spoonful of ice cream disappears into his mouth, and he shrugs instead of answering. Then he says, "I would have rather we'd stayed here. I liked it here, liked our house, my friends, my school. It's okay down there, but even after all these years, I still feel like the new kid. I guess that's why I really got into golf. It became my thing. And if I do well in this tournament, it will make a huge difference for me, since a spot on the team would also include help with tuition. I really need that."

I think about how important my own scholarships are to my family. It does make a huge difference.

"I can't even imagine what it would be like moving somewhere I didn't know anyone," I say. "My entire life I've been surrounded by family. Not a day goes by that I don't see at least half a dozen of them. Sometimes I think it might be nice to get away. Go where everyone doesn't know everything about you."

He rests his elbows on the table, his hands stretching out close to mine with his huge cup of mint chocolate chip between them. "And I just wish I could come back."

"But I guess change is coming for both of us. By fall, we'll all be somewhere new," I say, twirling my spoon through my ice cream.

"You know, the other night at Nonna's, I shouldn't have been surprised, but I was when I heard all of you are headed to LSU. I thought at least one of you would go somewhere else just to be different. My money was on Sophie, actually."

I laugh. "Yeah, she has a whole list of places she applied to. Charlie still gives her a hard time about it."

"So even though you're headed off to college, the gang will all be there," he says.

I lift one eyebrow, going for my sternest look. "We're not talking about the gang, are we?"

He tries not to smile but fails miserably. "No. We are not."

"Tell me some inside golf stuff. Something juicy," I say.

"Oh, the tales I could tell."

"Spill it!"

"Okay, so, this one time in eighth grade . . ."

We sit here for another hour while he tells me story after story. With the same group of people all showing up at the same tournaments over and over, of course there would be stories. Stories of parents cheating by throwing their kid's ball back in from the out-of-bounds areas, stories of hookups between players from different schools and the not-so-private locations these hookups took place. Stories of tantrums and runaway golf carts and fights. But also stories of nail-biting finishes and pranks at hotels and sneaking into country-club pools after hours.

"I think you found your family," I finally say. "Even though some of them sound like complete lunatics, they're your people. I mean, I'm surrounded by a few lunatics, too. Nothing wrong with it."

He seems to consider this a minute. "Yeah, I guess you're right. Never really thought about them like that. Just thought about all the things I missed at my school, like football games and parties on the weekends."

My face scrunches up. "Oh yeah, that's a little rough."

"Weekends are prime golfing time," he says, but doesn't look too torn up about it. "It's one reason I agreed to go to that party last night. I didn't want to miss out on everything."

"But you left early!"

He shrugs. "I'd been there long enough." Now he won't look at me. Instead he checks his phone and notices the time. "As much as I hate it, I really need to call it a night."

I'm standing up, grabbing my empty cup and spoon and taking them to the nearby trash can. "No, I'm with you. I have to be there at seven thirty in the morning."

Back in my car, we pull up in front of the Evil Joes' house.

"Thanks for the ice cream," I say.

"Thanks for ditching the band with me."

I gesture toward the house. "I could say something really funny right now, but I'm refraining, since it would break the off-limits rule."

Leo chuckles. "I can only guess. . . . Welcome to the gates of hell?"

"You said it! Not me!" I lean toward him and push his arm, laughing, and he catches my hand in his. He holds it there and then tugs me closer.

My heart is beating out of my chest when we meet in the middle, his lips on mine. He kisses me softly once, twice, three times before pulling away. I stop myself from grabbing him by the front of his shirt and kissing him again.

"Thanks for the ride home," he says quietly. And then he's gone. Jogging up to the front porch. I'm still sitting in my car stunned. Completely stunned. But there's also a ridiculously big smile stretched across my face.

I realize where I am and where I don't want to be caught if the Evil Joes come home, so I peel out of there like my butt is on fire.

It's only a few blocks to my house, but I make it in record time.

"Oh no," I mutter to myself as I pull into the driveway.

Charlie, Wes, and Sophie are sitting on my front porch, waiting for me. "Already finished watching Judd's band?" I call out to them once I'm out of the car.

"It was the drum solo that did them in," Sophie says, and then bursts into hysterics.

Now Wes is laughing. And Charlie, too.

"What happened?" I ask.

"Judd got a little overenthusiastic during his solo." Wes stands up and does an imitation of someone beating the drums. "And then he kicked one—you know the big one that sits on the floor? He knocked it loose and it hit the guitar player, pushing him off the stage. He was so busy holding up his guitar that he didn't try to break his fall."

"They had to call the paramedics. His whole face was bleeding," Charlie adds.

I can tell they really feel bad about finding it funny but also can't seem to stop. And now I'm laughing because they're laughing.

Then Charlie stops abruptly. "Wait. Where have you been? You left Superior almost two hours ago."

Sophie and Wes are waiting for my answer, too.

"Oh," I say, while my mind spins and spins for a believable story. "I went for ice cream."

Sophie's eyes narrow. "By yourself?" She knows the probability of that is low.

"No. Not by myself."

And now we're all staring at each other. It is a staring contest like we had when we were little. No one moves. No one blinks. They're waiting for me to tell them who I was with, and I'm trying to decide what to actually fess up to. I don't want to lie to them, but I also remember what Leo said outside Superior—*I like that this is just ours.* I'm not ready to give that up.

"You have to tell us," Wes says, his hand gesturing to the three of them. "You know this is killing us."

"A friend," I answer. I'm not lying. I very much think of Leo as my friend.

"A. Friend." Charlie enunciates each word. "What's this friend's name?"

"Someone I saw in the parking lot when I was leaving. We decided to go for ice cream." They're going to drag it out of me, but they'll only get a little piece at a time.

For some reason, though, Charlie likes my nonanswer. He jumps up from the front steps and exclaims, "Knew it!" He really doesn't know what he thinks he does.

My phone is vibrating in my back pocket, but I don't dare pull it out right now. If it's Leo, I don't want an audience.

I start up the stairs to the front door. "I'm heading to bed, since I have to be back out there in the morning." I stop and turn toward Wes. "Can you be here at seven?"

He groans but agrees.

"The party is a pool party at the same club as the golf tournament, so I can make an appearance there, I think. I can meet you to get my phone for a few hours, then we can swap back when the party is over," I say.

Wes looks relieved. "Oh, that makes it easy. Thought I was going to have to go in like Charlie and Sophie did."

"I can hang with you for a few hours until I have to head home," Sophie says as she wraps her arms around his waist.

"Good, because I think out of all of us, I'm the least quali-fied to act like Olivia to her mom."

Charlie heads down the front walk and turns toward Wes's house. "See y'all tomorrow," he says, leaving Wes to stay behind and say his good-byes to Sophie.

I head inside to give them a little privacy.

Once I'm in my room and in my bed, I pull out my phone and check my messages. I can't swipe open the one from Leo fast enough.

L: I had a really good time tonight
L: Can I see you tomorrow?

I let out a squeal and I'm glad no one is inside to hear me.

ME: I had fun too and yes I'd like that
L: How about an early dinner? Or a movie?

I start to respond, then remember the invitations hanging in the kitchen.

ME: Oh wait there's another grad party tomorrow night
L: Will everyone be there

I know who he's talking about when he says *everyone.*

ME: Yep! But maybe you can come too?

L: I'll be there

L: See you in the morning

ME: Can't wait

I stare at the screen a few minutes longer, but he doesn't text again. Pulling my blanket over my head, I replay tonight over and over. I fall asleep thinking about those three kisses in the car.

Truth #8: Ricky Bobby was right—if you aren't first, you're last

Thursday, May 12ᵗʰ, Morning

Olivia

I'm so exhausted. I'm so over the golf course. The only bright spot is seeing Leo, but it's not like I can talk to him. Which makes it worse. And I'm so tired of swapping phones and dodging Mom. I should just save myself the trouble. Tell her everything. Let her come home and tell me what to do. Let her fix it.

But I'm halfway through. Two days down, two to go.

Maybe today will be like yesterday and all I'll have to do is drive Mr. Williams around. Maybe I can put some earplugs in and ignore him completely.

Sophie is asleep next to me in the bed, so I slide out without waking her. I remember to pack a swimsuit, a cover-up, and a towel in my backpack for Megan and Lindsey's party. I feel like I'm catching a break with the party being so close. It should be easy to pop in and out, since it falls at the same time I took my lunch break yesterday.

My phone vibrates; it's Wes telling me he's on his way. Sophie sits up and grabs her phone, too, and I notice he actually sent it as a group text to both of us.

She stumbles downstairs, dragging a blanket from my bed with her, and curls up on the couch while I fix a cup of coffee to go. Wes drags himself in through the back door, still in pj bottoms and a T-shirt.

"Hey," he mumbles, half-asleep. He slides his phone across the table to me.

"Thanks, Wes," I say. "Mine's on the coffee table in the den. Sophie is on the couch."

I watch him walk into the den, then curl up around Sophie on the couch. She pulls the blanket over them both and within seconds they're asleep. Watching them sends a slight pang of jealousy through me, not only because of their relationship but also because they get to go back to sleep.

The drive out to the course feels like it takes forever and of course by the time I find a place to park, I'm fifteen minutes late. But Coach isn't there when I get to the clubhouse, and that feels like a miracle. Lily is waiting for me, though.

"Hey!" she says when she sees me.

How is she so perky this early in the morning?

"Hey," I answer. "Please tell me we aren't doing range balls this morning."

Lily frowns. "Sorry."

Following her to the closet that houses all the balls and trays and molds, I want to cry at the thought of spending the next two hours hauling buckets of balls and making those stupid pyramids. The only good thing is that I've finally become a pro at it and rarely have one that doesn't look great on the first try.

By the time we have each spot on the range ready to go, the golfers are pouring in.

My walkie-talkie crackles to life.

"Olivia," Coach Cantu says on the other end.

"Yes?"

"Drive a cart over to the delivery entrance of the clubhouse and pick up a couple of cases of water bottles."

"Yes, sir. On the way."

When I pull around to the back side of the building, there is a guy waiting for me standing next to the water.

"Where do I take these?" I ask.

"These are for the tournament guys. Take it to their check-in table."

He loads me up and I pull away. Wes's phone vibrates in my back pocket and I stop so I can check it while I've got a minute to myself.

I see my name on the screen.

"What's up?"

"You're on speaker with me and Sophie—" Wes says, then Sophie interrupts him with a loud "Hey!"

Wes continues. "We're calling to tell you that you have a message from L."

Uh-oh. "What's it say?"

Wes reads it aloud. "'Looking for you. I'm at the range.'"

I take a deep breath. "Is there anything else?"

"No. Is there anything you want to tell us?" he asks.

"Not at this time," I mutter. It's a miracle Leo didn't say anything that would give him away. I debated telling him about the phone swap, but that would only open up more questions about why I'm here, so yeah, I'm just winging it. Which I have never done in my life! And now I know why—it sucks to wing it. Too many things left to chance.

"Give us a hint! Please!" Sophie pleads. "We won't tell Charlie."

I roll my eyes. "Wes would totally tell Charlie and he knows it."

"Yeah, I'd probably break down and tell him. I would feel bad about it, though."

I need to go so I can deliver these waters and find Leo. "Okay, thanks for relaying the message."

Sophie jumps in before I can end the call. "Wait! Which

bathing suit did you bring? Your mom wants to know what you're wearing to the party."

"Ugh. Why does she care what I'm wearing to the pool?! Tell her the pink one."

"Wait, the pink one with the yellow trim or the pink one with the blue ruffle?"

"Yellow trim," I answer.

"Okay, I'll pass that along," Sophie says. "Better go find L!"

I end the call without saying bye.

It takes a few minutes to unload the waters, and then I'm hightailing it back to the range. From the tone of the text, it doesn't sound like Leo's just looking for me to say good morning.

I find him waiting for me, his bag on one of those push-carts. Leo is scanning the area and looks relieved when his eyes land on me.

This can't be good.

I pull the golf cart right up to him and hop out.

"Hey, what's going on?"

He's clearly concerned about something, but I still get a cute smile. "Morning. Wanted to see you before I teed off."

His hand reaches for mine and he gives it a squeeze. I squeeze back and resist the temptation to pull him closer.

"Also, need to warn you. Mae and the girls are coming to watch me play a few holes. There's some party at the pool here around lunchtime, so they thought since they were headed out this way, they'd come a little early. Mae just called me."

Oh God.

He must see I'm about to panic, because he adds, "I know you didn't want anyone to know you're out here. I tried to tell them not to worry about it, but they feel bad my parents aren't here to watch me play. I think my mom asked them to come. I'm sorry."

It dawns on me that while he may want their support while he plays, he told them no for me. And he doesn't even know why I'm hiding the fact I'm here.

"Please don't be sorry. I'm glad they're coming to watch you. Thanks for the heads-up. I'll be on the lookout for them."

He seems to relax a bit.

"This is the last thing you should be worried about. Seriously! I'm good! You go out there and kill it today," I say with the biggest smile I can muster.

And I mean it. If I know they're coming here, I'll just avoid them. At all costs!

His hand cups my cheek, his thumb stroking my skin. "I'm starting on hole three. Just so you know where we are."

I want to lean in closer. I want those three kisses again. It looks like he wants the same thing. There's a moment's hesitation before he moves his hand from my face. He pulls his hat off, the faded blue one he's worn the past two days, and drops it on my head.

"Maybe you can hide behind this if they get too close," he says.

I put my hand on the brim, about to pull the hat off and hand it back to him. "No, I can tell this hat means something to you. I can't take it."

But he stops me from removing it. "I'll like knowing where it is."

I lean in before I can talk myself out of it and give him a very quick kiss on the lips. "Good luck today!" Then I hop back in the cart and pull away.

I park the cart behind the supply room and go back to refilling range balls. With Leo gone, my panic comes back full force. I am a nervous wreck. Everywhere I go includes a quick check of the area to see if Aunt Maggie Mae and the Evil Joes are nearby. I don't take two steps without looking around in each direction. It's madness.

An hour later, all the golfers have finished warming up at the range and everyone is about to tee off. I find myself back in the cart with the fun-sucker, Mr. Williams.

Aunt Maggie Mae and the Joes make an appearance not long after we get started. They have rented a cart and all three of them have squeezed onto the bench seat. They fit right in, since they're decked out in gear just like the female players, bows and all for the twins.

I stuff my hair inside Leo's hat and pull the brim down low. My sunglasses hide half my face and I'm praying they don't recognize me, mainly because they aren't looking for me to be here.

Mr. Williams has directed me to hole four, the one Leo should be on right now, so I hunch over in the driver's seat, hoping the bare minimum of me will be visible. Mr. Williams is looking at me weird, and I get it. I'm trying to disappear into the small steering wheel.

"Pull up right over here and stop."

We are literally feet from where Aunt Maggie Mae is parked. Great. Thankfully, Leo's attention is fully on his game.

Leo lines up his shot, doing that same little ritual he does at the range. He looks down at the ball, then out to where he wants it to land, several times before settling his gaze back on the ball. He pulls his club back and then lets it go in a beautiful swing. The club connects and the sound echoes through the trees.

I don't know how they know where the ball lands because I lose sight of it the second it's airborne. But by his expression, Leo seems pleased.

Aunt Maggie Mae starts clapping and yells, "Great job, Leo!"

Mr. Williams is about to lose it, I can tell.

"Excuse me, but you must be silent while you are on the

course!" He's amazing at whisper-yelling. I've witnessed it a number of times over the last two days.

Aunt Maggie Mae spins around to find out who would ever dare try to tell her what to do. I duck in the opposite direction and become very interested in the grass growing next to the back tire.

"Well, excuse me. I'm just letting my son know I'm proud of him!" she says.

Her son. I roll my eyes. I'm sure she thinks if she's related to him, she gets certain privileges. But I could have told her every parent here thinks they get special privileges.

They do not.

"This is your only warning. The next time I have to remind you of the rules of the tournament, you will be asked to leave."

I expect Aunt Maggie Mae to fire back, but she must really be worried he'll kick her out. Next time I'm around her, I need to channel my inner Mr. Williams.

We stay with the players on this hole until they've all finished on the green.

"Hole six."

Yesterday we went to all the holes in order, but it seems like today we're only going to the even ones. I guess there's a method to his madness, but I haven't figured it out yet.

Honestly, I'm happy with whatever makes the day go faster.

Just as I'm about to hit the gas so we can get out of here, I chance a quick look at Leo. He's pulling his cart with his bag toward the next tee. He nods at me. I nod back and throw in a big smile.

Phone Duty: Wes

I wake up on the couch alone.

"Where'd you go?" I mumble. "Come back."

Sophie chuckles from the direction of the kitchen. I smell coffee and cinnamon and that's all it takes to get me up and moving.

She's in front of the oven, pouring melted icing over cinnamon rolls, when I come up behind her, wrapping an arm around her waist. "That smells delicious."

"I figured we couldn't go to Nonna's for breakfast without Olivia or that would look suspicious."

"Good call."

Olivia's phone is on the counter and it's lighting up.

"Is Aunt Lisa texting already?" I ask.

"Yep," Sophie says, laughing. "Started about thirty minutes ago. I told her which bathing suit Olivia will be wearing and now we're discussing cover-ups."

I move away from Sophie and head to the coffeepot, fixing

myself a cup. "You're so much better at this than me. Are you sure you can't stay with me all day?"

She turns her head, looking at me over her shoulder, and I'm blown away by how lucky I am that she picked me.

"You know I can't. I have to get to Minden to help set up for the party tonight. And you have to meet me there as soon as you switch phones with Olivia. The party starts at six."

"I won't be late." Sophie spends a lot of her spare time in Shreveport with us, so I try to make sure we spend time in Minden with her friends, too. I know she misses them, especially Addie.

Her ex-boyfriend, Griffin, tried to make things difficult for me at first, but when I didn't respond to his games, he finally quit playing them.

"Who's going to man her phone tomorrow?" I ask her. "It's going to have to be Charlie, since we're staying in Minden tonight." Whenever we're there, her parents let me spend the night in the guest room so I don't have to drive back. The first time they let me stay, her dad and I had A Talk. One that scared the crap out of me, especially since he's the sheriff. But since then, they've always made me feel at home.

"Yeah, it'll have to be him. You tell him."

I throw my hands up. "Nope. That's Olivia's job."

Olivia's phone vibrates and I grab it before Sophie does. "I need to practice while you're still here to check my work."

But it's not from Aunt Lisa.

L: Looking for you. I'm at the range

"Oh, well, well, well," I say.

Sophie is peering over my shoulder. "What?"

"Ah! It's that Locke guy! Call her and tell her!"

We call Olivia, and she's as evasive as she was last night about who she ate ice cream with. Like we didn't know she was with him!

"We're going to have to get to the bottom of that," I say, smirking, and Sophie agrees with me.

We hang out at Olivia's until it's time for Sophie to leave. I walk her to her car out front and linger there for a minute. I can't wait until we're living in the same town this fall.

"I'll see you in a few hours," she says. She's behind the wheel and the window is down. My hands are braced on the roof of the car.

"I won't be late."

I lean in and give her one last kiss good-bye, then watch her drive away.

Olivia's phone vibrates in my pocket as soon as the car disappears around the corner.

MOM: Don't forget your sunscreen. You're still recovering from that burn earlier in the week.

That's not too bad. I can handle this.

ME: It's already in my bag

MOM: Perfect! And how are you doing your hair?

Okay, this is a little trickier. I move to Olivia's front porch swing and try to remember what she normally does with her hair. I mean, it's long. And sometimes it's kind of curly.

ME: I may braid it

I don't know what Charlie is complaining about. This isn't hard.

MOM: I bought you some more cream for razor burn. You know how bad it gets around the bikini area. It's in the middle drawer in my bathroom.

Nope. Nope, nope, nope, nope. That's it. I'm out. Not even responding to that.

☀ 🖤 ☀

Olivia

OLIVIA: I'm here

I'm in the women's locker room changing into my suit and cover-up when Wes texts me from my phone. My hair is thrown into a loose bun and I put on a little lip gloss. Thank God I remembered to shave this morning.

Slipping on my tennis shoes since I forgot sandals, I jog out to the parking lot to meet Wes.

He's parked near my car with his windows down and his seat reclined. The smell of fast food hits me when I get close.

"Hey," I say.

"Hey." He hands me my phone through the open window. "Your mom was chatty this morning."

There's something in his tone that makes me worry what she could have possibly said to throw him off. Compared to Charlie, Wes is hard to rattle.

"Judd's been texting you all morning." I hand him his phone. "Thanks for doing this."

"Anytime. I'll be waiting out here until you're done." He points toward the burger and fries he has spread out on the bag in the passenger seat. "But I do need to be headed to Minden by four. Sophie has her grad party tonight."

"Yeah, that shouldn't be a problem."

Walking back to the clubhouse, I check my phone. No new messages from Leo.

The pool sits on the opposite side of the clubhouse from the driving range. There's a brick fence and gate closing it off from the parking lot, but the back is open to the course. I've seen it when we lap the holes, and I'm pumped for the chance to enjoy it for a bit.

There are big gold balloons in the shape of the numbers of our graduation year attached to the gate. Most of the girls are already here when I get to the pool area. Megan and Lindsey greet me by handing me a towel with my initials monogrammed on it and a beach bag with my name. Both are super cute.

"We're so glad you're here," Megan says.

"Yes! There's food on the table over there." Lindsey points to a long table behind them.

"Thanks so much for inviting me!"

They move on to greet the girls coming in behind me, and I spot Bailey and Mia on lounge chairs not too far away. I drop my stuff on the empty chair next to Mia.

"We had bets whether you'd be here or not," Bailey says. "You've been curiously absent all week."

"I know. It's been crazy. You have no idea."

Mia pulls her glasses down to look at me. "We'd have an idea if you filled us in."

"I will, but right now can we just soak up the sun?" I have about twenty-four minutes before I have to be back to work. There's no way they're going to let me skip out of here without a good excuse.

God, I'm so tired of this.

More girls show up, including the Evil Joes, who apparently had their bikinis on under their golf-watching clothes.

They sit on the loungers on the other side of the pool while Aunt Maggie Mae takes an empty spot at a table under a big umbrella with the other moms here.

This party is laid-back, and if I wasn't checking my watch every five minutes, it would probably be my favorite. I would stay in this chair all day. Pull an umbrella up when my skin turned pink. Drink frozen drinks until I got a brain freeze.

About fifteen minutes in, Megan's and Lindsey's moms call out for us to gather around the shallow end of the pool. There are only a few people here who aren't with the party and most of them are mothers with their young babies in the baby pool. The only students out of school right now are seniors, but I can imagine how packed this place will be once everyone is out for the summer.

We gather around the end of the pool and see lots of blown-up inner tubes, the kind that are shaped like animals. There's a flamingo and a frog. A yellow duckie and a unicorn. A bull and a llama. And on and on.

"Time for party games!" Megan's mom yells, and half us of groan while the other half cheer.

Lindsey's mom holds up a few gift bags. "And prizes for the winners!"

Now some of the groaners have moved to the cheering side.

"For our first game, here's what you do. Everyone picks a

float! Sit on it any way you want. The first person to make it to the other end of the pool is the winner!"

I don't know if I'm more worried about this game or the fact that it's only the *first* game. I check my watch once more. I don't have much time at all.

There is a mad dash for the pool floats. I'm one of the last ones to pick and I'm stuck with the giraffe. His head is so tall I'm going to have trouble seeing where I'm going and I'm worried it's going to be top-heavy.

There are so many of us that we stretch across the entire shallow end of this gigantic pool. Some girls are sitting with their butts in the opening, their legs dangling out, but that's a poor choice. Some are lying across the whole thing, while others are straddling theirs in a really awkward sort of way.

I go for lying across mine. That way I can kick and paddle at the same time.

Megan's mom is at the edge of the pool, holding a green flag up high. "On your mark! Get ready!" There's a short pause and then she finishes, "Go!"

And we're off. It only takes a few minutes to determine that the ones lying across their tubes made the best choice as we break away from the crowd. Looking at my competitors, I see there are only five of us in this position. And of course, the Evil Joes are two of the five.

What can I say? Our family has always been competitive.

We are loud as we compete. Some of the golfers on the hole nearest to the pool have stopped what they're doing and turned around to watch us. I'm sure Mr. Williams would have a stroke if he were here.

I kick and paddle and kick and paddle, edging into the lead. But then here comes Mary Jo.

We are in the battle of our lives. I'm sweating and my arms are burning and I can hardly feel my feet anymore, but I will not let her beat me.

From the way she's moving, she feels the exact same.

Some of the girls who never got off the starting line have left the pool and are now at the finish line, cheering us on. I hear both of our names in the noise and I feel like I need this win more than anyone even knows.

We are so close to reaching the edge of the pool. Mary Jo and I are neck and neck. At the last possible minute, I throw myself off my tube, my hand touching the edge before I go face-first into the water.

I swim up, breaking the surface, looking for the official ruling.

Mary Jo is clinging to the edge, still on her tube, and saying, "That doesn't count! She left her float!"

I'm treading water, since this is the deep end. My giraffe has floated away and left me to die. "My legs were still on it when I touched the edge!"

Megan's mom and Lindsey's mom are huddled up discussing it. I'm sure they didn't expect such a cutthroat ending to their race.

They talk and talk and nod at each other then finally turn to us. "That ending was too close to call, so it's a tie!"

"What?" Mary Jo yells while I shout, "A tie? Seriously?!"

The moms ignore us. "Let's move on to the next game!"

I glance at Mary Jo and she's looking at me.

"That wasn't a tie," she says. "I won fair and square."

I roll my eyes. "I beat you and you know it."

We both drag ourselves out of the pool and follow everyone else. My legs are Jell-O. I notice she's limping a little, too, and that brings me some satisfaction.

We catch up with the crowd but realize it's not all fun and games anymore. There are several tournament officials in their monogrammed golf shirts talking to the moms.

I hear the words "noise level" and "distraction" and I know where this is going. And then I catch sight of Coach Cantu.

And he catches sight of me.

I'm supposed to be working off my time, but instead he's caught me dripping wet in a two-piece and causing a distraction to the golfers.

This is not good.

He nods for me to come to where he is and I slowly make my way to him. I glance behind me and notice Mia and Bailey are clued in that I'm in some sort of trouble, but they obviously have no idea why.

"I'm sure you'll give me some explanation as to why you're swimming instead of working, but I don't want to hear it. You have five minutes to be dressed and back out on the course, or we can forget this whole thing and you can head home."

He turns away and walks with the tournament guys out of the pool area.

I'm a little pissed at first because technically I'm on my lunch break, but then I look at my watch. My lunch break ended ten minutes ago.

I rush back to my lounge chair and scoop up my belongings, thankful for the bag and towel. There's no time to even say bye to Megan and Lindsey. Bailey and Mia watch me from the other side of the pool, but I'm gone before they can make their way over. I sprint to the women's locker room and throw on my other clothes while I'm still damp. My shirt and shorts are sticking to me and my hair is sopping wet. I pull it up into a bun and slide my tennis shoes back on.

I'm out the door with seconds to spare.

Coach is waiting for me.

"I'm really shocked I even have to say this to you, but this is your last chance. If you can't do what I've asked, there's no reason to continue."

He huffs out a breath as he heads toward the range.

I feel terrible and I want to bang my head against the wall.

And then I remember Wes in the parking lot.

"Hey," he says after the first ring.

"Hey," I say. "I got busted by Coach at the party and he's pissed. I can't go out to the parking lot right now. Will you meet me at the clubhouse to switch phones?"

"Yeah, sure, on the way."

While I wait for Wes, I act like I'm busy by picking up left-behind water bottles and putting them in the recycling bin. Mr. Williams is off to the side, talking with some of the other officials, and I know at any minute, I'll be back to driving him around.

The second Wes comes into view, I rush to where he is. We switch phones again and he asks, "How much longer do you need me to stay?"

I shrug. "You can leave now. I don't care anymore. If Mom asks, just say I have a headache and I'm going home to nap. And if my friends start blowing up my phone trying to figure out why I disappeared, just ignore them. I'll text them back later. In fact, turn my phone off. I really just don't care."

Wes puts a hand on my shoulder, which prompts me to look up at him; his face is full of concern. "Are you okay?"

"I'm fine. It's fine. I just need this to be over."

He hesitates a second, but there's nothing more he can do. He's already doing so much. They all are. I got myself in this mess, so I'll have to get out of it.

"Okay, well, call me if you need me. Even if it's just to talk."

My eyes get misty and I'm afraid I'll break down at any second. "I'll make sure I'm home by four so you're not late for Sophie's party."

Wes leaves and I want to sit on the ground and never move. But Coach will surely banish me for that, so I walk toward Mr. Williams and wait for him to tell me he's ready to hit the course again.

I stand there patiently, but Mr. Williams isn't in any hurry. My eyes wander around the area and I see Leo off to the side, next to the now-vacant check-in table. All his clubs are out on the table and he seems to be rearranging his bag.

I judge the distance between us and weigh the pros and cons of going to talk to him. He's only a few feet away and I will hear Mr. Williams the exact moment he calls for me. And Coach has ridden off in his cart, so he's not around. And it's not like I'm talking to Leo while he's playing.

"Hey," I say when I get close. "How's it going today?"

He stops what he's doing and turns toward me. "Hey! It's going pretty good, actually." He moves in closer, his hand reaching out, and I'm not sure if he wants to touch me or hold my hand or pull me to him, but I'd be good with all of the above. He stops midway as he remembers where we are, and his hand falls to his side. "I've managed to shave a few strokes off my game today." He tilts his head to really look at me. "Is your hair wet?"

I scrunch my face up. "Yep. Made an appearance at the party at the pool."

"Ah!" he says. We both glance in the direction of the pool even though we can't really see it from here. "I'm guessing Mae and the girls are still over there."

"Yeah, at least for another hour, I think."

"But you couldn't stay the whole time?"

"This feels a lot like you're asking an off-limits question." I just know he'll hear about the inner-tube race from Mary Jo later, but I don't want to waste what little time I have with him talking about her.

He puts his hand to his chest. "I would never!"

I wave toward the table that has all his clubs and things on it. All of them with that neon-green grip, except for one in the middle. "What are you doing?"

"Rearranging my bag. Mae and the girls bought me a new club as a gift and I'm trying to make room for it."

"Oh, that was nice of them," I say. I mean, look how nice I am, giving them a compliment.

He ignores the clubs and focuses on me. "What's the grad party tonight? I don't have to dress up in a costume, do I?"

"No. It's a scavenger hunt."

"Like we have to go into the woods and find sticks and leaves?"

"No, not like that. Someone did this party for a group of girls a few years ago and it was a hit, so now every year someone has The Scavenger Hunt. There are teams and you go around town and do things. And you post it to your team's Instagram account so everyone can see what everyone else is doing."

He steps a little closer. "Like what kind of things?"

I shrug. "Well, I don't know what we'll have to do tonight, but last year, they had to do things like go in front of Starbucks and sing 'I'm a Little Teapot.' With the dance and hand motions and everything. It was fun watching the team accounts last year."

"I bet," he says, laughing.

"Olivia!"

I spin around when I hear my name. It's Mr. Williams. I clutch Leo's hand, giving it a big squeeze, then say, "The fun-sucker calls. I have to go. I'll see you tonight!"

And I'm sprinting away before he can say anything else.

I skid to a stop in front of Mr. Williams and he hands me a stack of papers. "Can you go inside the office and make a copy of these? And then I'll meet you back out here."

I nod, accepting the papers. The copier is ancient and it takes forever, but after about fifteen minutes, I have the task completed. Mr. Williams is right where I left him, talking to the same group of people. I take a quick moment to check if Leo is still at that table but he's gone.

But there's a single club leaning up against the table. Its handle is neon green.

"Oh crap!" I mutter to myself.

I go to pull my phone out to call him but remember I have Wes's phone instead of mine. It's not like I've memorized Leo's number. I don't see him anywhere, but finally I spot his bag sitting in his pushcart right by the tee box for hole ten.

I only have a few minutes before Mr. Williams will be ready, so I grab the club Leo left behind and run like wild to the bag, dropping it inside.

And then I haul it back to Mr. Williams. He's turning around looking for me the second I get back.

I hand him the papers and he motions toward the golf cart.

"Ready?" he asks.

I nod. "Yes, sir. I'm ready."

Just as we're about to pull away from the clubhouse, Leo walks out of another door, a bottle of water in his hand. I raise my hand and give him a small wave, hiding the motion from Mr. Williams. He returns the wave. He's smiling big and there's pep in his step. I'm thrilled he's playing so well today.

And how cool will it be if he's playing for LSU this fall! I could go watch his matches, cheer for him from the sidelines— quietly of course.

Wait. Am I thinking about long-term things with Leo?

I am. I really am.

It's dumb to think a couple of days of flirting are going to amount to anything serious. I haven't seen him in years!

It's ridiculous.

Thinking about him makes me happy. So maybe that's something to build on.

But it's not something I can worry about right now. I have to focus on getting through to tomorrow afternoon without completely screwing up. Again.

Phone Duty: Wes

I'm leaving the clubhouse area when I run into Locke. Charlie told me last night after Olivia left that he was supposed to show up at Superior, and Charlie's convinced that's the "friend" Olivia got ice cream with.

"Hey, man, what's up?" I say as I'm about to pass him.

"Hey, Wes, what are you doing here?" he says.

"Just bringing Olivia something she forgot at home," I say, glancing back at the area behind me. "How's it going?"

He loses the smile. "Okay. Could be better. I was hoping for a top-five finish, but doesn't look like that'll happen."

I wince. "That sucks. Sorry to hear it."

"It is what it is. Lots of good players here this week. There's this guy from St. Francisville who is killing it. He's playing better than he's ever played. And I've played with Leo for years. Wasn't expecting it."

This throws me. "Leo?"

"Yeah. Leo Perez. Do you remember him? He went to school with us when we were younger."

"Uh, yeah, I know him. Didn't know he was playing, though." And honestly kind of surprised Olivia never mentioned it.

"Yeah, he's got a chance of finishing top three."

I put my hand out and he shakes it. "Well, good luck. Hope you can pull it out."

"Appreciate it," he says.

I'm just about to walk away when I turn back to him. "Did you hear Judd's in a band?" I ask, laughing because I can't not laugh when I say *Judd* and *band* in the same sentence.

"Yeah, I saw on someone's story the other night that he let loose on his drums! I would have loved to have seen that."

We both laugh and head in separate directions.

When I'm back at Olivia's, I start thinking about the whole L thing. So I text my phone.

ME: I ran into Locke at the course when I was leaving.

Olivia doesn't answer right away, but it doesn't take too long.

WES: Oh. Okay
ME: He said Leo Perez is killing it out there

Those three dots jump around a lot longer than they should and I can almost picture Olivia typing and deleting and typing again.

WES: I saw him like once yesterday. From a distance. I hear he's doing pretty good but I don't know

Yeah, she's full of it. I'm thinking the *L* in Olivia's phone may not stand for *Locke* after all.

SCAVENGER HUNT!
for
ANNIE, ARCHER, & ELLA

May the Best Team Win
Thursday, May 12th
5:30 PM, Riverside Park

Truth #9: I really, really, really like Leo Perez

Thursday, May 12th, Evening

Olivia

I'm driving like a madwoman. I'm sweating and on the verge of tears.

Coach made me stay late to make up the ten minutes from lunch and the fifteen minutes I was late the other morning.

I called Wes to tell him I would be getting back after four and I could hear the disappointment in his voice as he said it was okay—a very different tone than the teasing one earlier in the texts about Locke and Leo.

And it's not okay. They've done everything I've asked of them and all Wes needed was for me to be on time today.

I screech up in front of my house and barely put the car

in park before I'm jumping out. With my hand outstretched, I pass off Wes's phone to him and take mine back.

"I'm so sorry," I say.

He barely looks at me. "It's fine. But I need to go."

My face crumples and I lie down in the grass as his car races away. I can feel the tears leaking out of the corners of my eyes.

Picking up my phone, I send Sophie a quick text.

ME: It's my fault he's late. Coach made me stay late. I'm so sorry.

A quick scroll through my messages shows me Mia and Bailey are perturbed that I'm not answering them as to where I ran off to. My fingers hover over the screen as I try to decide how to reply. But I don't. I can't. I mean, what am I supposed to say that isn't another lie?

It takes a while for Sophie to text me back, but when she does all I get is: ok

Ugh. Why am I screwing up every single thing?

"Are you dead?"

I lift my head to see Charlie walking down my driveway. My head flops back down and I say, "I wish."

"I heard a little about it." He drops down on the grass next to me.

"How mad is Wes?" I ask, unable to hide the catch in my voice.

"Nothing he won't get over. You know how he is."

There's a big lump in my throat. "He's too nice for us."

"Whatever. So why are you out here wallowing in self-pity? What else happened?"

"Everything."

Charlie is pulling out blades of grass and throwing them at me, but they blow away in the breeze before they land. "When Wes got back from the club, he said he ran into Locke."

I close my eyes and pray for the earth to open up and swallow me whole.

"He didn't say much else about it, but I can read Wes like a book and there's more to that. Any idea what it is?" Charlie asks.

Now I kind of wish the earth would swallow Charlie up so this conversation would end. "No idea."

"Okay. Good talk. Better get a shower, because you're driving me to the party. We're leaving in an hour and a half."

As Charlie scrolls through his phone in the passenger seat on the way to the scavenger hunt, I let my mind wander to Leo. I've texted him a couple of times to see how he finished the day, but I haven't heard back. Hopefully he'll be there with the Evil Joes and I can figure out how to talk to him without Charlie having a fit.

I still have a pit in my stomach over making Wes late, though. It doesn't seem to be going away, even after seeing pics of them at Sophie's party where all looks well.

We get to the park and there's already a big group of people here. The moms hosting have a check-in table set up near some picnic tables, so we head that direction.

Bailey suddenly pulls me aside. "You disappeared again! And you haven't responded to a single one of my texts. What's going on? We saw you talking to one of those golf guys."

I think about what to say, an excuse on the tip of my tongue. But I'm tired of lying to her. And while I still can't bring myself to admit that my graduation is on the line, I can tell her part of it.

"I've been helping with the golf tournament. Coach Cantu, who taught my off-campus class, is in charge and I'm making up a few of the classes I missed by working it."

Mia walks up just then.

"Where have you been?" she asks.

Bailey repeats my explanation and they both look at me, confused.

"That's what you've been doing all week?" Mia does not look convinced.

"Yeah, that's it."

"But you said you were working at your grandmother's shop," Bailey says. "Why would you lie?"

And this is where it gets hard because technically, Sophie is the one who lied for me, but I'm not dragging her into any more of this than I have to.

"I was embarrassed. I'm sorry."

I can tell they aren't quite buying it.

The moms call everyone over, so I'm spared—for the moment—having to answer any more questions. Bailey and Mia are a little frosty to me, which is no less than I deserve. Looking around, I notice the Evil Joes have arrived, but I don't see Leo anywhere. Why isn't he with them? The last thing we talked about was him meeting me here.

"Okay, everyone! It's time to play!" one of the moms yells. "We're going to draw names for teams. Each team has a captain, and captains are in charge of taking the pictures and videos and uploading them to the team's Instagram account. This is how we'll monitor if you've completed the challenges and also give your competitors a glimpse as to where they stand. You will have one hour!"

The moms start pulling names out of a big jar and I take a second to try to call Leo again. It goes to voice mail. I'm instantly worried something bad has happened, but the Evil Joes wouldn't be here if he were laid up in a hospital somewhere, would they?

I hear my name called and I turn around.

It's Mia.

"You're on the green team," she says. I walk to the table and one of the moms hands me a bright green bandanna. It reminds me of Leo's golf clubs.

She points me in the direction of the green-bandannas group. I'm on a team with four other people: Archer (one of the seniors this party is for), Judd, Danlee, and a guy named Mason. I wish one of the golfers was on the team, but I haven't seen any of them here yet. At least I'm not stuck with the Evil Joes.

"Okay, group huddle," Archer says, motioning us to come in close. He holds out a piece of paper. "Here's the list. We need someone to keep us on track and someone to drive."

"I'll drive," Judd offers, and we all veto him.

Danlee says, "I'll drive." No objections.

"I'll keep up with the list." I need a distraction.

The moms get our attention once more. "You cannot speed or break any laws. You must respect others' property. If you need a stranger to help with a challenge, that stranger can only be used once!" She then gives us the go-ahead to start and we race to Danlee's car. Once we're in and on the road, I skim the list.

1. *Charlie's Angels* pose with two strangers and a team member

2. A team sitting with a family/group enjoying their yummy meal
3. Entire team's reflection in something other than a mirror
4. Entire team doing a handstand
5. Entire team at a fire station (+1 if in front of or inside of a fire truck)
6. Entire team with a stranger wearing a concert T-shirt (+1 if the stranger is playing air guitar)
7. Entire team playing Twister—without a mat
8. Two members pose in the front window of a store as mannequins. ASK FOR PERMISSION FIRST!
9. A human pyramid involving at least one stranger
10. Find a stranger wearing a T-shirt with the logo of a team member's future college and take a pic with stranger and team member
11. Two team members challenge a pair of strangers to a three-legged race—must run at least fifteen feet and use your bandannas to join the legs
12. Entire team going down a slide (+1 if the slide is a spiral slide)
13. A team member inside a restaurant kitchen washing the dishes
14. Interview a stranger outside the movie theater about the movie they just saw—must ask the name of the movie and at least two questions (+1 if they give you their ticket stub)

15. Team playing one round of Duck, Duck, Goose at the Duck Pond
16. One teammate dances in front of a stranger, and the stranger scores them on a scale of 1–10
17. Team saying the Pledge of Allegiance in front of an American flag
18. Do exactly what a sign says (any sign will work)
19. Reenactment of any scene from a Will Ferrell movie
20. Get advice from a stranger

"Who came up with this?" I mumble.

"Where am I going?" Danlee asks.

I direct her to the park everyone calls the Duck Pond not far from here. There are several things we can knock out if we can find an open grassy area.

She pulls into the parking lot next to the park and we jump out.

Skimming the list again, I say, "Okay, let's start with Duck, Duck, Goose!"

Mason will video and Judd has volunteered to be the one to start the game, so Archer, Danlee, and I sit in a tight circle on the grass.

Judd walks very slowly around us, patting us each on the head as he says, "Duck."

"You know this isn't a real game," Archer says. "Say *goose* already."

But Judd is Judd and the game continues. Finally he pats me on the head and yells, "Goose!"

I jump up, ready to tag him and move on to the next item, but he is running for his life. Finally, Danlee grabs his leg when he passes her and holds him for me so I can tag him.

Another team arrives and I see Charlie and Mary Jo were both picked for the red team. We are never going to hear the end of this.

We knock out the handstand task and the slide one quickly, then look for a willing stranger to dance in front of.

"I've got this one!" Judd says.

He picks this mom who's pushing her little girl in a stroller. But Charlie runs up to her at the same time.

Charlie and Judd lean in and talk to her for a second and she nods, agreeing to whatever they've just asked her. She clearly doesn't know them.

Judd pulls out his phone and we hear music playing. Oh my God, it's "SexyBack" by Justin Timberlake. And they are both dancing to it. In front of this poor mother.

Again, this challenge needed about ten seconds of dancing and then her score, but Judd and Charlie are in a full-on dance-off.

The red team is on one side and we're on the other, each cheering for our teammate. Charlie is the clear winner, but I stay loyal to the greens. Even when Judd's on his third round of the Sprinkler.

Now the little girl is dancing in her stroller and clapping for the guys. The dance-off is being filmed by both sides and I can imagine the moms laughing when it's uploaded.

This song is longer than I remember.

I think Charlie and Judd agree, because they finally call it quits about halfway through. Both are gasping for breath.

The mom claps for both, then leans down to chat with her daughter, who can't be older than three.

"Who was the best one?" she asks the little girl.

The girl's eyes get big and her gaze bounces from one boy to the other. She finally points to Charlie and yells, "Him! Him! He rolled on the ground!"

The red team cheers and everyone is hugging everyone else until it's Mary Jo and Charlie's turn. They don't hug but they do high-five, which is REMARKABLE for them.

We run through several more tasks that can be done at this park, including Danlee and me challenging two middle schoolers to a three-legged race. Mary Jo and her teammate Destiny join in, but Danlee and I smoke them and it feels good.

By the time we've left the park, we've got almost half of the list done, but we've also burned up about half of our time.

We head to one of the busier streets to find a restaurant for the "doing the dishes" and "eating with a family" challenges. Judd and Archer head inside with Danlee and Mason so they can film it. I stay behind, outside the building, and try Leo one more time.

He finally answers on the fourth ring.

"Yeah?" he says, his voice flat.

"Oh my God, are you okay? I've been worried to death! I thought you were coming to this party!"

He's quiet for what feels like forever, then he finally responds, "It's not a good time."

I pace around in a tight circle while I talk. "Do you want me to come over? Or pick you up so we can go somewhere to talk?"

"No. No, that's where I went wrong this week. I'm here for the tournament and nothing else. I've had Mae and the girls driving me nuts and then I got distracted with you," he says. I flinch at the tone of his voice. "And for what? Now it might not even matter. None of it may matter."

I feel like I've been punched in the stomach. "Where is this coming from? Did something happen?"

"Look, it's been a pretty shitty day. Tomorrow doesn't seem like it's going to be any better. And I'm tired. Really tired. I need to go."

The line goes dead just as my group comes running out of the restaurant, laughing hysterically. They're already rehashing what happened inside, but I can't hear them. I feel like I'm underwater and everything is muted. We get through the rest of the challenges with zero help from me. Danlee asks a couple of times if I'm okay and I wave her off. I can't even talk.

And then, replaying the conversation with Leo, I start to get mad. Really mad. I don't know what happened, but I don't deserve that.

We get back to the park just as the hour is up. My team turns in our sheet and we relax on one of the picnic tables while we wait for all the other teams to get back and for the moms to tally up the scores.

I toss my phone from side to side, thinking of all the things I want to text him. But I don't.

The party rolls on around me. Other teams are arriving and everyone is exchanging funny stories of things they had to do.

But I'm stuck in that conversation with Leo.

Finally a group that includes Lily shows up and I sprint to where she is.

"Hey, Lily," I call out. Lily is the only one from the golf course I've seen here so far. "Did something happen with Leo Perez at the match this afternoon?"

She grimaces. "It's bad," she says. "Really bad."

I step closer. "What happened?"

"He may be kicked out of the tournament."

Kicked out! He's close to winning it!

"Why?" I croak out. I feel the tears gather in my eyes.

"He had just finished the last hole and from what I heard had his best game ever. But then he called an official over.

I could tell something was really wrong. He and the official talked for a few minutes, then Leo started pulling all his clubs out, laying them on the grass."

"But what does that mean?" I ask.

"He had too many clubs in his bag. You're only allowed fourteen, but he had one extra."

My stomach drops. Does this have something to do with the club he left leaned up against that table? The one I went and put back in his bag?

"That's a rule?" I shriek. "That's insane."

Lily shrugs. "He knows it's a rule, though. He told the officials he rearranged his bag and left one club out after putting a new one in. He said he left it on the check-in table for a family friend to pick up and take home. He said he has no idea how it made it back into his bag."

I screwed it up. It's my fault. It's all my fault.

"You said he *may* get kicked out. What do you mean?"

Lily lets out a slow breath. "He called it to the officials' attention. He didn't have to. In fact, he probably would have gotten away with it, since he was basically done for the day. He told them he doesn't know how it got in his bag. Normally, they would disqualify him immediately, but they're talking it over and will let him know in the morning."

"Why would he tell on himself like that? That's so dumb." Then I'm shaking my head. It's not dumb. It's honorable. And that's who Leo is. I've heard enough. I'm sick to my stomach at what I've done. If I'd read that whole rule book, I would have known that was a rule. A big one. But I didn't. And it may cost him the tournament. And a place on the LSU team, along with all that scholarship money.

Because I thought golf was stupid and it didn't warrant any of my time or attention.

I find Charlie hanging out with Bianca. The moms have set food out and Charlie and Bianca are sitting down, eating.

"Hey," I say, leaning down so only Charlie will hear me. "I need to go. Can you catch a ride home?"

"Are you okay?" he asks because it is obvious I am not.

"Yes, just need to go."

The tears are in full force by the time I get home. Sophie is in Minden at her party, so I can't call her with this right now, especially since she's probably still mad at me, too. And as much as I want to call Leo back, I don't even know how to begin to tell him what I did.

He's never going to forgive me.

And I don't blame him.

The
Great Shreveport Bake Off

Let's bake and celebrate
Bianca Bandini

FRIDAY, MAY 13TH,
WHISK DESSERT BAR

2 PM

Truth #10: This is the most Friday the
13th of all Friday the 13ths

Friday, May 13ᵗʰ, Morning

Olivia

I'm outside the country club before it opens. It was dark when I got here. Sleep eluded me. I think I may have only gotten about three hours, since I couldn't quit thinking about Leo and what I did. The damage I caused.

Charlie texted me at some point last night asking if I was okay again and if he needed to be on phone duty today, since Wes and Sophie are still in Minden. I haven't responded to him yet. My phone is still on the charger on my bedside table so Mom won't see where I am.

I wait in my car until I see the tournament officials pull up. They arrive in unison, all five of them in their matching polo shirts and khakis, ready for the final day of play.

By the time they reach the check-in table, I'm right behind them.

"Excuse me," I say. "Can I please talk to you a minute? It's really important."

Mr. Williams comes forward, since he's the only one who knows who I am. "What's wrong?" I must look a mess, because there's actual concern on his face.

Tears fill my eyes and I brush them away. Mr. Williams gestures for me to sit in one of the chairs while the other officials casually gather in the remaining chairs or perch on the edge of the table.

"I need to tell you what I did yesterday. I'm the one who put the extra club in Leo Perez's bag."

This gets their full attention.

Mr. Williams leans forward in his chair. "Why don't you start at the beginning."

I probably go a little too far back, since I start by telling them how I know Leo and his relationship to the Evil Joes, but I'm proud of myself for calling them by their real names.

"It's just, I don't know anything about golf. I thought it would be an easy class. A blow-off. And they handed me a rule book when I started on Tuesday, but I didn't read it all the way through because I thought . . . why would I need to know the rules when I'm not playing?"

I'm crying hard now that I'm getting to the part about what I did.

"My aunt Maggie Mae bought Leo a new club as a gift. And she gave it to him here, in the middle of the tournament," I say, rolling my eyes. "As much as I don't know about golf, even I wouldn't expect someone to use new equipment for the first time in the middle of a tournament as important as this."

One of the officials hands me a paper towel and I'm grateful, since I'm one step from wiping my nose on the sleeve of my T-shirt.

"But Leo is such a nice guy. He didn't want to hurt her feelings, so he rearranged his bag to make room for it. I walked up while he was doing that right here at this table." I look at Mr. Williams. "You were off to the side, talking to some other men, and I was waiting to drive you around. It was right after my lunch break. You asked me to make a copy of some papers, which I did."

He nods like he remembers the time frame I'm talking about.

"I knew something was wrong with Leo last night, but it wasn't until I found out what happened that I put it together. He asked my aunt and cousins to pick up the extra club once they were finished at their party. He would have had to tee off before they were done. So he left it sitting there, hoping they would grab it for him, since they were at that pool party. You know, the one that was so loud yesterday."

All five of them shake their heads and mutter things like "Oh yeah" and "That one" and "So loud."

"I came back out here after making the copies and Leo was gone, but his pushcart and bag were just over there." I point to the area between here and the tee box for hole ten. "He must have gotten his bag back in order and gone in to use the restroom before heading back out. But I saw one of his clubs leaned against this table. And I knew it was his because it had the same neon-green handle. And I assumed he overlooked it when he was putting everything back in his bag. So I grabbed it and ran to his bag, dropping it in with the others. I thought I was helping."

I'm hunched over in my chair so far that my head is almost in my lap. But I sit back up because I need to finish, as painful as it is.

"That's why he had no idea how it got in his bag. And my family probably thought one of the others grabbed it."

The officials are all looking at each other now. I have no idea if they had already come to a decision about what to do with Leo, but if they were planning to disqualify him, I pray I've swayed them in some way.

The gray-haired guy on my right says, "It's very clear you are upset about the part you played in this. We appreciate you coming forward and telling us what happened. We will take everything you've said into consideration."

That's it? How can that be it? I confessed! They have to know he didn't do it on purpose.

"You aren't disqualifying him, are you? It's all my fault, not his."

Mr. Williams responds, "We will make a final decision this morning. Even though he wasn't the one who put the extra club in his bag, each player is ultimately responsible for the contents of their bag." He must see I'm about to go into a full-fledged meltdown, because he adds, "The best thing Mr. Perez has going for him is that he brought it to an official's attention the moment he discovered it. That says more about him than anything else. And you certainly cleared up the 'how it got there' part."

"Leo is an honorable player. He doesn't deserve to get thrown out over my mistake."

Mr. Williams nods. "We're taking all of this into consideration." He pauses a moment, then adds, "But I think it's best if you're not on the course today."

My head falls. I knew this was a possibility. I mean, if they didn't kick me out of here, Coach Cantu would have. Especially after yesterday at the pool.

"Will you please tell Coach Cantu what happened and why I'm not here?" I say.

"Yes. I'll let him know."

I get up from my seat and walk slowly back to my car.

Looking back, I see they're sitting down around the table in deep discussion, probably deciding Leo's fate right now.

But my fate is sealed. By not finishing today, I don't get my hours. And there's no way Coach Cantu will sign my form after what I've done.

I get in my car and drive to the only place I can think to go.

Nonna's house.

I creep in through the back door in case they aren't up yet, but the smell of coffee and bacon hits as soon as I enter.

Poking my head around the corner, I see Nonna at the stove.

"Hey," I say, quietly.

She startles but recovers quickly. "Olivia! What a nice surprise!" And then she sees my face. "Oh, sweet girl, what's wrong?" She turns off the fire under the pan and has her arms open just in time to catch me. I bury myself in her embrace and the tears start rolling once again.

Nonna walks me to the one of the stools at the counter and sits me down but doesn't release me. She lets me cry without saying a word, just rubs her hand down my back over and over. This somehow makes me cry harder.

When I finally catch my breath, I pull away from her. She sits down on the stool next to me, her hands clasping mine.

"Want to talk about it?" she asks quietly.

"I screwed up. So bad."

She reaches over and hands me the box of tissues off the counter and I pluck three out quickly.

"Like *We'll have to visit you in jail* screwed up? Maybe I can bake a file in one of my cakes. Help you bust outta there."

Chuckling, I wipe my eyes and nose because everything is leaking.

"Not quite jail-time bad," I clarify. "But bad. And not just for me. I may have screwed up something important for a good friend."

"But you don't want to tell me what it is?" she asks. Her tone hints she already knows the answer.

Groaning, I say, "You'll find out soon enough."

She gives me a squeeze and a kiss on the top of the head. "Well, let's get some food in you. That will make you feel better."

Nonna heads back to the stove and turns the fire back on. In seconds, the bacon is sizzling again. She fixes me a cup of coffee and slides it across the counter to me. I don't know how, but she can fix any member of this family a cup of coffee and it will be exactly the way they like it.

There's a pan of biscuits that goes into the oven, then she's cracking eggs into a skillet.

"Want me to help?" I ask.

"No. Just relax. Drink your coffee. Clear your mind."

And that's what I do. I get lost in watching her move around the kitchen. The same room she has fed this family out of for fifty years. She and Papa bought this house right after they got married. It was big but in bad shape and Papa got it for a steal, he likes to say. They lived on one side while they fixed up the other. Then they switched. All eight of her children were brought home from the hospital to this house. All of her grandchildren have run through this kitchen.

I'm lucky to be a part of this family.

It's not long before Uncle Michael and Tim show up.

"Olivia!" Uncle Michael says when he sees me. He crosses the room to give me a hug. My red puffy eyes are a dead give-away. "What's wrong?" His tone is serious as he drops onto the stool next to me. I glance at Tim, but he's moved closer to Nonna to wish her good morning. Probably giving us a little privacy to talk.

"Tough day," I say.

He searches my face. "Already? Can I do anything?"

Shaking my head, I say, "No, but I'll be okay."

"You will. No matter what's going on, it's only temporary. Work through the problem, find the solution, and fix it."

I wish it were that easy.

Tim brings Uncle Michael a cup of coffee and gives me a soft smile. I'm grateful he doesn't ask me why my face looks like this.

"Okay, you can make a plate," Nonna announces.

You'd think with only three of us in the kitchen, one of whom has been crying her eyes out, it wouldn't be a mad dash to the front of the line. But it is. Uncle Michael and I jump up at the same time and knock each other out of the way. He pulls me back by my T-shirt so he can get in front of me, but I stick my foot out and poke him in the stomach, which startles him enough that he lurches to the side, giving me back my lead. We're both laughing and pushing and laughing some more, but by the time we get to the stack of plates Nonna has out, Tim has beat us there by calmly walking around the other side.

"Amateurs," he says while Nonna piles food on his plate.

I elbow Uncle Michael in the side. "I like him."

Uncle Michael's face lights up. "Me too."

When other family members start showing up, I sneak out the front door and head back to my house, leaving my car at Nonna's since it's blocked in by Uncle Sal's and Uncle Marcus's.

I head straight to my room and bury myself under my covers. With a full belly, a somewhat clear conscience, and only a few hours of sleep last night, I'm dead to the world within minutes.

"There she is! Thank God!"

"She's sleeping!"

"That coach is going to be pissed she overslept."

I hear the voices and know that it's Charlie, Sophie, and Wes, but I can't seem to pry my eyes open.

Then Charlie jerks the comforter off me. That does the trick. I sit up in bed, my hair going every direction and my eyes swollen,

"Why'd you do that?" I moan.

They all three look speechless.

Charlie recovers first. "We've been calling you for hours! You never told us who needed to be you today. And then you didn't respond or answer your phone, so we got worried."

Sophie sits down on the edge of the bed. "But your car is at Nonna's, so we stopped there first. She said you were there for breakfast."

"Did you get out of going to the golf course today?" Wes asks.

Flopping down on the bed again, I try to pull the comforter back over my head, but they won't let me. Sophie crawls into the bed and settles in next to me on my right. Charlie plops down on my left. Wes is on the other side of Sophie.

"Tell us what's wrong. You're never like this," Sophie whispers.

I look at her and Wes. "I'm so sorry I was late yesterday.

You've been so perfect this week and I screwed up the one thing that mattered to you."

Sophie hugs me tight. "Oh my God, I hope you don't think we're mad at you."

"God, oh no, we're all good!" Wes says.

"What else is going on?" Charlie asks. "You're not this upset over that."

And I spill it. All of it. I start with talking to Leo the first day when he walked me home from Nonna's house. I don't skip anything . . . not how I feel about him and not how I screwed things up for him. And for myself by getting banished from the course.

It takes forever for me to tell the whole story. It feels like weeks. It feels like years.

They are quiet when I finish. And still. No one moves and no one speaks.

For a long time.

Finally Sophie asks, "So you don't know if Leo was disqualified or not?"

I shake my head. I'm not sure I have any words left in me.

"Well, hell," Charlie says. He pulls out his phone and makes a call, putting it on speaker.

A girl answers. "Hey! What's up?"

I recognize Lily's voice.

"Hey, are you at that golf tournament?"

"Yeah, why?"

"Can you tell us if Leo Perez is still in it?"

When he says *us*, Lily knows that's me.

"Yes. They let him stay."

Tears race down both cheeks, I'm so relieved. I look at Sophie and she's crying, too.

"Okay, thanks. Uh, how's he doing today?"

There's a muffled groan. "He's had a rough morning. There were a lot of parents who challenged the ruling. But the officials weren't having it. I think it messed with his game."

I pull Charlie's phone out of his hand. "Can he make it up? He just needs to finish in the top three."

"Maybe. He'd have to play this afternoon like he played yesterday."

I'm about to hand Charlie his phone back, but I ask one last question. "Does he know it was me?"

"Yes, the officials told him about your visit this morning."

I drop the phone in Charlie's lap and burrow back down in my bed. Sophie scoots even closer to me.

Charlie thanks Lily and ends the call. We're all quiet once again.

"So, what does this mean for graduation?" Wes asks.

I shrug, but I'm so buried in these covers they probably don't see it. "Coach was so pissed at me about the pool party yesterday. Said that was my last warning. The tournament officials said they were going to tell him what happened and why I was asked not to be there for the last day of the tournament."

Charlie asks, "Have you checked your phone? Maybe he called you. Or texted."

We all look toward my phone sitting on the nightstand.

"I don't want to look," I mumble.

"I'll look," Charlie says, and I yell "No!" and roll over to hold him down.

He gives up easily and we go to back to just lying there.

After a few minutes, Sophie says, "Just look. It's killing me."

"I second that," Wes says.

"Third," Charlie shouts.

"Okay, fine. I'll look." I lean across Charlie and grab my phone but hold it low so no can see the screen. It lies on my chest, facedown, my hand resting on top.

"You. Are. Killing. Me," Charlie says, enunciating each word.

I take a deep breath, then blow it out while I bring the phone up so I can finally see the screen.

There are lots of notifications. From Mom, Charlie, Wes, Sophie. I swipe open the phone so I can see all my conversations. First thing I see is a text from Leo.

L: Today is pretty shitty. Hard to sort through all of it. But thank you for clearing everything up

"Aww," Sophie says.

"What?" Charlie lifts his head so he can look at Sophie on the other side of me. "Why is that an *Aww* text?"

"Because!" She props herself up on her elbows so she can see him, too.

Charlie looks at me. "What's your call on it?"

I'm still staring at his words. "I think he could have been ugly to me and I would have deserved it. I think he's struggling today and even though he still gets to play, I'm the reason why it's hard. And although I cleared things up, he's playing poorly and that's due to my actions. He still may not get his scholarship."

Charlie drops his head back down on the pillow next to me. "Even if we like him now, we do not have to like the Evil Joes. They are not a package deal."

I squeeze Charlie's arm. It's a big move for him to let this go with Leo. "It might not be an issue. He may not want anything to do with us."

Now it's Wes's turn to sit up. "Of course he does! What's not to love?" And then Sophie pulls him back down.

Exiting out of the conversation with Leo because I want a little time and privacy before I text him back, I scroll down and see a text from Coach Cantu, which is shocking, since I've yet to see him use a phone. It's from nine o'clock this morning, about two hours after I spoke with the tournament officials.

Beside me, Sophie takes a deep breath when she sees. "Open it!"

I really don't want to do this with an audience, but these people know everything. They should know this, too.

COACH: You leave me no choice. I am unable to sign your form since you have not completed your hours.

Well, there it is. Surprisingly, I'm not crying. I guess I'm all cried out.

"He sucks," Wes says.

"Call Mr. Spencer. Tell him what happened. He can overrule that guy."

Thinking back to the e-mail exchange with our vice principal earlier this week, I say, "He can't. I already asked him. He said no."

"I'm so sorry," Sophie says. She rests her head on my shoulder.

"It is what it is." I feel hollow inside.

My phone rings in my hand and it startles us enough that we each scream.

Mom's name flashes across the screen.

"Are you going to tell her?" Sophie asks.

"Not right now. I can't handle any more today."

I swipe the call open and put it on speaker.

"Hey, Mom," I say, hoping my voice doesn't sound as sad as I think it does.

"Hey, sweetie! How are you?" She is cheery. So very cheery.

"Good, just hanging out with Sophie, Wes, and Charlie."

"Wonderful! Well, good news! Dad and I are on the way home! We got done late last night and we are on the road. Should be there right after lunch."

I want to let out the loudest groan right now, but I don't. I hold it together. Because now my plans of wallowing in bed all day are shot.

"Oh, good!"

"Can't wait to see you!" Mom says.

Sophie leans close and whispers in my ear. I shake off her suggestion but then decide it's not a bad idea after all.

"I may be at that party for Bianca when you get home. It's at two, I think."

"Aw, that's right! Well, we'll see you after! Love you!"

She ends the call, and I turn to Sophie. "The last thing I want to do is go to a party," I say.

"We're not staying in this bed all day. We're going to Bianca's party and making a cupcake. The sugar will do us good. And then you can face your mom when we get back."

I sigh and say, "Okay. But I'm showering before I do anything."

"Yes, please do," Charlie says, and I punch him in the arm.

The three of them get out of the bed to head downstairs.

"Party is in a couple of hours," Sophie says, then shuts my door behind her.

I ignore my phone but pull out my laptop from the drawer in the nightstand. I hesitate a second, then grab Leo's faded blue hat and slip it on. I may not deserve it, but I feel better once I'm wearing it.

Pulling up LSU's website, I start researching while thinking about what Uncle Michael said—work through the problem, find the solution, fix it. I can't fix what I did to Leo any more than I already have, but I can see what my options are, since it doesn't look like I'm going to graduate next week.

I scroll through the site and read every FAQ page I can. When I can't find a definitive answer to what I'm looking for, I break down and call the admissions office.

"LSU Office of Admissions. This is Tess," a woman says when the call connects.

"Hey, I have a quick question. I've been accepted to LSU for this fall, but I may not have my diploma until midsummer because it seems like I'm missing a half credit of PE. If I can take it this summer, would that affect my standing for the fall?"

"Oh, you should be fine. As long as all your high school

credits are met by the time classes start in August, you're good to go."

So that's it. I thank her and end the call. It could be so much worse. I'm still going to college this fall. I'll still get a little money in scholarships, although I'll be missing a big one by not graduating as salutatorian. That's going to be the hardest part when I admit everything to my parents.

The lost money makes me think of Leo. Grabbing my phone, I pull up our conversation again.

ME: I can't tell you how sorry I am. I thought I was helping but I ended up hurting you. And that kills me. I'm so, so sorry.

I throw down my phone and head to the bathroom.

Charlie, Sophie, and Wes are waiting for me on the front porch when it's time to leave for Bianca's party. Charlie holds out his phone. "Switch with me," he says.

"What? Why?"

"Charlie and I are going to the cupcake thing for Bianca while you and Sophie go to the golf course," Wes says.

Backing up a step, I shake my head. "No. I can't."

Sophie pulls my phone from my hand and gives it to

Charlie, then hands me his. "Yes, you can. We checked with Lily. The match will be over soon. They'll tally the scores, then the winner will be announced in about forty-five minutes. We're going to be there for Leo."

I blink the tears away. "He won't want me there. Coach won't want me there. The officials will lose it if they see me there."

"They can't do anything else to you. The awards ceremony is open to family and friends. That's what we are."

Sophie starts to pull me to her car, but I resist.

"Hold on," I say, then sprint back inside. I grab the blue ball cap and put it on, pulling my ponytail through the small opening. And then I'm back outside.

"This is a bad idea," I say, when Sophie's car pulls away from the curb.

"We're full of bad ideas. So what's one more?"

The entire ride to the course has my stomach in knots. Sophie and I are quiet and the only sounds in the car come from the radio station. I think she's as nervous as I am.

The guard at the entrance of the country club starts to give her a problem until I lean forward and wave. He lets us through. What a difference a week makes.

"Gosh, there's a lot of people here." Sophie circles the parking lot twice and only finds a spot after someone leaves.

Getting out of the car, we walk side by side. I have a strong urge to grab her hand for support, but instead I take a deep breath and throw my shoulders back. I have every right to be here.

We bypass the clubhouse and walk around the building until we're on the back side, where the big board showing everyone's daily score is. Today's numbers haven't been put up yet. There's also a podium there now, along with a microphone and a table full of trophies.

Sophie wants to get closer, but I grab her arm, holding her back. "This is far enough." I'm happy I'm here, but I don't need to be front row.

The golfers are in a cluster on the far side while the parents are standing right in front of the trophy table. Coach Cantu is nowhere in sight.

Mr. Williams approaches the podium and checks the mic before saying, "First, I'd like to welcome all of the parents and friends who are here to support our golfers. We could not do this without all of you! And we'd like to thank Ellerbe Hills Country Club for allowing us to use their incredible facility. And thanks to the weather for cooperating!"

A low chuckle rumbles through the crowd. I've been keeping an eye out for Leo since the moment we arrived, and I finally spot him when the guy in front of him leans over to pick something up.

He looks exhausted. After what Lily said about some

people being mad he wasn't disqualified, I was worried he'd be off by himself, but he's got a group surrounding him. Tears spring to my eyes when I see him.

Mr. Williams's voice booms out, "It's my honor to present the trophies and awards for the winners of this year's tournament! It's been a wonderful three days and I'm very excited for the future of these golfers."

He shuffles his papers and a ripple of nervousness and excitement races through the crowd. Yesterday Leo killed it and was sitting in first place going into today. I hope he was able to get his game back.

Mr. Williams starts with the girls and I'm thrilled to hear Tanika got third place. She's beaming when she walks up to accept her small trophy.

Now it's time for the guys.

"In fifth place is Christopher Locke."

Everyone claps, including us.

"In fourth place is Kenneth Jung."

I squeeze my hands together in prayer. Leo needs to make top three to get his scholarship. My eyes are sealed shut and I chant silently, *Top three, top three, top three.*

"Third place goes to Jason Reiner."

My stomach sinks. Lily said he was doing bad this morning. I was thinking third place would be a miracle. And then Mr. Williams says, "And in second place is Leo Perez."

There are a few mumbles and groans, but they're drowned out by the cheering. And most of the cheering for him is from the other players. Well, Sophie and I are doing our part as we scream and jump up and down.

Part of me wonders if Leo could have held on to first place if he hadn't had to deal with all the drama last night and this morning, but by the look on his face, he's ecstatic. He takes the trophy from Mr. Williams, then leans in to say something to him. Mr. Williams pats him on the shoulder and Leo heads back to his friends.

"Oh, there's Aunt Maggie Mae," Sophie whispers. Sure enough, she's here, along with Uncle Marcus.

Mr. Williams awards the first-place winner, but we've tuned him out.

Now the parents are converging on the players, congratulating the winners on their game.

"Do you want to go say hi to him?" Sophie asks.

I shake my head. "No. Let him enjoy this. I'm just so relieved he finished well."

There's a man in a purple golf shirt with the LSU logo walking up to him. They greet each other and shake hands. Leo is grinning big when the man hands him an LSU cap. Leo takes off the random hat he's wearing, replacing it with the one for his new team. I can't help but touch the brim of the blue hat he gave me a few days ago.

I start walking to the car with Sophie reluctantly following me.

"Are you sure you don't want to at least wave from a distance? He won't even know you were here."

Not looking back, I say, "I'm sure."

We pull away while we can still hear the sounds of the
players celebrating.

Phone Duty: Charlie

Wes and I crash Bianca's party right as it's starting.

The party is at a local bakery and the girls are set up
at stations in the large kitchen. The chef welcomes everyone
from the front of the room.

"Hey," I call out, waving to Bianca.

She jumps up from her stool and makes her way to us.
"What are y'all doing here?"

"Olivia is checking out the results of a golf tournament her
friend is playing in and hated that she was going to miss your
party. So we're here in her place!"

"Well, can't say I mind you showing up. Let me get y'all
some aprons," she says, clapping her hands together.

Within minutes, Wes and I are in pink ruffled aprons,
mine monogrammed with Olivia's name and Wes wearing one

monogrammed with the name *Susie*. Susie, we discover, is Bianca's cousin who woke up not feeling well this morning.

The chef, a guy named Blake, is at the front of the room, holding up items and telling us what they're for.

"Oh, we're totally going to kill this," Wes says. He's a pretty good cook, which has worked out well for me over the years, since I'm always hungry.

Wes and I follow the directions Blake gives us and our cupcakes are baking before anyone else's.

We high-five and do a victory dance near the ovens.

"Seriously, Charlie, you've been to more parties this week than Olivia has," Mary Jo says.

I saw the Evil Joes were set up on the other side of the room when we first got here and was hoping I could avoid them. No such luck.

"Why is Olivia at the golf course? Who does she know out there playing?" Jo Lynn asks.

Wes grins and replies, "Leo Perez."

And I wish I had a picture of their faces when Wes said his name! That mix of shock and disgust would be my screen saver. I would send it out as Christmas cards.

"Why are they out there watching him?" Mary Jo screeches.

"Why aren't y'all?" I ask.

Jo Lynn looks like she wants to go for my throat. "Mom and Dad are there. We offered. He said he didn't want us to miss our party for that."

For that. For the most important tournament of his high school career. We should have convinced Leo to defect to our side years ago. I'm finding I like Leo even more now that I know the Evil Joes hate us being friends.

"Yeah, okay," Wes says, then walks back to our station. I just give them *a look* and follow him.

Wes has his phone out and says, "He came in second!"

Hell yeah. "Maybe Olivia won't be so hard on herself now."

Wes laughs. "You know how Olivia is."

Yeah. I do. She'll hold on to this for a long time.

Her phone vibrates in my pocket, so I pull it out and see a notification from L. I flash the screen at Wes and he raises his eyebrows.

"You opening it?" he asks.

I give him a look like he's crazy. "Of course I'm opening it."

L: Heard you were here

"Don't reply," Wes says. Then rolls his eyes. "You're going to reply."

ME: This is Charlie. I have Olivia's phone. Long story. But we all hope you'll be at the crawfish boil that our family is throwing for us tonight. We figured you'd get invited by the Evil Joes but you also have an invite from us too

"Aw, look at you being all sweet," Wes says, and I punch him in the arm.

The timer on his phone goes off, letting us know our cupcakes are ready. "C'mon," he says. "We have a cupcake competition to win."

CRAWFISH BOIL

honoring

Charlie Messina
Jo Lynn Messina
Mary Jo Messina
Olivia Perkins
Sophie Patrick

Friday, May 13th, 7 pm
Greenhouse Flower and Gifts

Dare #1: Tell the truth

Friday, May 13th, Evening

Olivia

Mom and Dad are home when we get back from the golf course. I'm hugged and kissed on the cheek, and it takes all my willpower not to blurt everything out, but I don't want to put a damper on the party Nonna and Papa are hosting tonight. I'll confess after it's over.

Mom sits at the kitchen table with a cup of tea and says, "Okay, tell me all about it! I hate that I wasn't here this week. I know you had so much fun at all the parties!"

Sophie and I join her at the table and give her just enough detail that she's satisfied. Charlie and Wes pop in not long after. Charlie and I trade phones when Mom turns away to put her cup in the sink.

"Well, I've got to get changed and get to the shop to help everyone prep for the party tonight. I feel bad—they've been working all week and I'm just gonna waltz right in," Mom says.

"Yeah, we need to get ready, too," Sophie says.

Wes moves toward the door, motioning for Charlie to join him. "We told Nonna we'd help, too, so we'll see y'all there." They leave and Sophie heads upstairs to get dressed, but I hang back to talk to Mom alone.

"Can we get rid of the tracking app now?"

I can tell she's struggling with her answer. She likes the inside peek into my life, though she never treated it like a *Gotcha!* where she was trying to catch me doing something wrong. "Yes, of course," she says with a smile. "It was just for the week, wasn't it?"

I move closer to her, giving her a big hug. "I'm glad you're back." And I mean it.

She hugs me back fiercely. "I can't believe you're graduating next week. And then the house will be empty."

Mom is going to be devastated when I tell her the truth. I pull away quickly.

Sophie is in the shower when I get upstairs, so I lie on my bed, scrolling through my phone, until she gets out and I can get in.

And that's when I run across Charlie's texts with Leo. Sitting up in my bed, I overanalyze Leo's message for ten minutes.

Heard you were here

Is it like *Heard you were here and I'm so sorry I missed you!* or more like *I heard you were here—haven't you done enough already?*

I can't even be mad at Charlie's text. I knew Leo would be at the crawfish boil tonight unless he decided to go home straight after the tournament, since the party is for the Evil Joes, too.

I hope he's there.

Sophie comes out wrapped in a towel and I slip into the bathroom. By the time we're dressed and ready and heading to the car, I still don't have a grasp of what tonight will be like. Or what it will be like to see Leo.

Pulling up in front of Nonna and Papa's shop, Sophie and I are both speechless. By rearranging the plants and trees in stock, they've created a wonderland. There are crape myrtle trees strung with lights lining the front walk and pots spilling over with flowers on each step.

"This is gorgeous!" Sophie sighs at last.

I couldn't agree more.

We follow the lighted path through the shop and out the back door. It's really an old house that's been converted into a business, and the big backyard is a perfect place for all the plants.

Normally a maze of pots and shelving, the plants have been grouped around the edges so the entire center is open.

is a cooking trailer in the very back where the crawfish are being boiled, and tables set up with red-and-white-checkered tablecloths. The party is for family and friends and doesn't officially start until seven, but Nonna and Papa wanted all the family here early so it could be just us for a bit.

Except for the Evil Joes, Sophie and I are among the last to arrive. The entire area is full; I don't know how the other guests are going to fit in here.

"Here we go," Sophie mumbles as we make our way over to greet each and every family member.

Aunt Patrice and Uncle Ronnie are the first we come to. She hugs us both at the same time while Uncle Ronnie pats us on the head.

Aunt Patrice pulls back from the hug and zeroes in on me. "We are so proud of you, Olivia! Salutatorian!" She turns to Sophie. "We're proud of you, too, sweetie." Then they walk off.

"She's still not over it that I bailed on that living Nativity," Sophie says, and I can't help but giggle.

Moving farther into the party, we find Aunt Kelsey and Uncle Will. They have four daughters and you never see either one of them without at least one kid hanging off them.

"Girls! Happy graduation!" Aunt Kelsey says, pulling each of us in for a one-armed hug since she's got Frannie on one hip and Mary hanging on to her leg.

"We're so proud of you both," Uncle Will says. Birdie is

sitting on his shoulder and Gracie clinging to the front of him. "Do you give a speech, since you're salutatorian?"

"Uh, yeah, the welcome speech," I answer, feeling about one inch tall.

"Can't wait to hear it!"

Sophie's parents and my parents descend on us next. Mom has her phone out and she's taking pictures as they reminisce about when we were babies and how they're going to be empty nesters now and just go ahead and shoot me.

Aunt Eileen pulls me in close and whispers, "We couldn't be prouder of you, Olivia!"

And that's it. I can't take it. I'm a fake. A fraud. I'm not salutatorian. I'm not even a graduate.

Sophie must see it on my face because she whispers, "No, no, no, not yet."

But it's too late for that. At least telling them now will be like ripping the bandage off.

Walking to the nearest chair, I pull it to an open area and stand up on it. "Can I have everyone's attention, please?" I yell.

Nonna claps. "Aw! Are we getting a preview of your speech?"

Ugh.

"No, Nonna, but I do have something I need to tell everyone, and since everyone is here, this seems like the right time."

Uncle Michael moves a few feet closer as if he knows I'm going to need a hug once this is over.

"As most of you know, I take school very seriously." There are claps and cheers throughout the crowd, but I hold my hands out and they quiet down.

"I wanted to take as many AP classes as I could, but I didn't schedule everything right. By the beginning of this last semester, I realized I still needed half a credit in PE. But I also wanted to take Law Studies, so I thought, I'll just do off-campus PE. And I chose golf." From their expressions, they're clued in that this is not going in the direction they thought it was. "But I didn't give it the time or attention it deserved. I missed too many classes. So this past week, I've been working a golf tournament at the new country club right outside of town, trying to make up my hours."

Mom's confused, trying to figure out how I was in two places at once. I will definitely hear about this later.

"But I screwed up there, too. I thought I was helping someone, but I really messed up because I didn't understand the rules. They asked me to leave. And I didn't finish my time there, and my coach won't sign my form, so I won't be graduating next week with everyone else."

Everyone is talking at once now.

"I'm sure we can talk to your coach," Dad says. "What's his name?"

"The school can't stop you from graduating just because of PE, can they?" Aunt Patrice asks.

"I'll call up to that school," Uncle Sal says. "I know a guy up there."

I clear my throat, quieting them down again. "I can take the class over this summer. It won't affect my admission to LSU. It's okay."

Stepping down from the chair, I'm hoping that will be the end of it. But it's not. Not even close. My grandparents, my parents, my aunts and uncles, and even some of my cousins surround me to offer suggestions or condolences or to just plain commiserate. It's twenty minutes before there's only Charlie, Wes, and Sophie around me.

"That was harder than I thought it would be," I say, rubbing a few stray tears away.

Sophie wraps me in a big hug. "I think it was very brave."

"I'm sorry you won't be graduating."

I turn around to see who said that, and it's Leo. He's back in the clothes he was wearing when I first saw him at Nonna's, but he's got the LSU golf team hat on.

Charlie, Wes, and Sophie congratulate him on his tournament finish and then make themselves scarce, leaving us alone.

"Is that the reason you didn't want to tell me why you were working the tournament?"

"I was embarrassed. I mean, I work so hard for four years

and the whole thing comes down to a PE class?" I let out a nervous laugh. "I guess you heard all that?"

"Yeah," he says. "If you hadn't told them how the club ended up in my bag, they wouldn't have asked you to leave and you'd have gotten your hours."

"That wasn't even a choice. There's no way I could let them kick you out for something I did." I pause a moment, then add, "I'm really so sorry."

He's shaking his head. "It's the stupidest rule out there. I'm sorry I was a jerk last night. I shouldn't have taken it out on you."

I give him a friendly push against his chest. "Hey, it was my fault."

He grabs my hand and keeps it there, pressed up against him. I feel his heart beating as fast as mine. "But I didn't know that then. All I knew was you were the only thing I was thinking about when I should have been thinking about my game, and I was mad at myself."

"I was pretty distracted by you, too."

"Thanks for inviting me to your party," he says.

Frannie wedges herself in between us and whispers, "Hide me!" But Dallas and Denver see her and now they're chasing her as she runs circles around us.

I'm having the most romantic moment ever and I'm completely surrounded by my chaotic family. I can't catch a break.

Once my cousins move on to another target, I slide my

hand into Leo's and say, "I'd like to reintroduce you to my family."

He gives me a smile and says, "I'm not promising I can remember everyone's name."

"It would be a miracle if you did," I say, laughing.

I pull him to Uncle Michael and Tim, who are standing closest to us. They shake hands and talk about golf. Turns out Tim played in college, too.

Leo and I are stuck together like glue. We even spend a little time talking to the Evil Joes, although I know I'll hear about it from Charlie later.

I scan the crowd looking for him. He's at a small table with Bianca. Their heads are bent close together and his hands are clasped in hers. I watch them for a few minutes and wonder if he's rethinking his "free to mingle" plan.

"Olivia!"

Turning, I see Mia and Bailey have arrived. "Be back in a second," I tell Leo.

I pull the two of them off to the side, where we can talk. "I'm so sorry I lied to you this week. There's really no excuse. I'd like to tell you what happened."

And I do. I go through it with them just like I did with my family. And when they're just as understanding about it all, I realize I'm as lucky to have them as I am to have Sophie, Wes, and Charlie.

"We'll just have to have another round of grad parties once you finish your summer-school PE class!" Bailey says.

"Oh God, no," I moan.

"Are you taking something new?" Mia asks.

I smile and look back over my shoulder to where Leo is talking to Charlie and Wes. "I'm sticking with golf. I know this guy who can tutor me, so I should be all good."

Saturday, May 14th

Leo and I are in the hammock in the backyard of my house, lying at opposite ends so we're facing each other. There's a gentle breeze, and the shade from the giant trees makes the heat bearable.

I had a long talk with my parents last night. Mom was really upset when she found out we tricked her with the phone. And a little embarrassed that she couldn't tell she was texting Wes and Charlie instead of me. I mean, Sophie she understood, but that the boys fooled her was more than she could handle.

It was a long night. Once the interrogation was over, I went upstairs and finished the stupid questionnaire. Even though the school won't be looking for it, Nonna texted that I still owe her a copy for her box. And I gave myself permission to write *Undecided* for as many of the answers as I wanted.

I felt really good.

"What's the plan for today?" Leo asks.

I stretch my arms out wide. "Absolutely nothing! Isn't it glorious?"

He squeezes my ankle. "Works for me."

We swing back and forth, slowly. I don't know what this thing is between us and for once I'm not trying to figure it out. He's staying for the graduation ceremony and then he'll head home the next day.

"Do you regret not walking in your graduation?" I ask him. His school held their ceremony this past Thursday, but he missed it for the tournament.

He shakes his head. "No. Like you said the other night, my friends were on the course with me. Most of them missed their graduations, too." He shifts slightly, propping himself up on my legs. "And I made some new friends this week."

My grin is ridiculous. It's all teeth. I should be embarrassed but I'm not.

I tug on the blue baseball cap. "So what's the story with this hat, and are you okay that I'm never giving it back?"

He pulls me a little closer and I let out a squeal. "First time I played golf after I moved to St. Francisville, I was wearing that hat. It was brand-new. Mom bought it since it was in the colors of my new school. A guy whose dad is friends with mine invited me to go play. And I fell in love with the game. And did surprisingly well for a beginner. From that point on, whenever I played, I wore that hat."

I go to pull it off and hand it back to him. "I can't keep it. Not when it means . . ."

He stops me, covering my hand with his as we both slide it back on my head. "I told you. I like knowing where it is."

I'm saved from saying something cheesy when my phone rings. I lean to the side to pluck it off the ground and almost tip us over in the process.

I'm laughing when I answer. "Hello?"

"Miss Perkins?"

I recognize that voice. Mr. Spencer.

"Yes, sir?" And now I'm struggling to sit up, which is hard to do in a hammock. I'm squirming around and Leo is trying to help me without really understanding what I'm trying to do.

"I received your e-mail this morning and I'm a little confused. Are you turning down the salutatorian honors? You've asked me to find a replacement for you to give the welcome speech."

"Um, well, I figured if I wasn't graduating, I couldn't give the speech."

I had e-mailed Mr. Spencer late last night after the long conversation with my parents, telling him that since I would not be salutatorian, he'd need to give the next person in line notice so they could start working on what they would say.

"I mean, I didn't get the off-campus PE form signed and you said there was nothing you could do if he didn't sign it, so . . ."

"I got your form yesterday afternoon," he says.

This stops me cold.

"Yesterday afternoon?"

"Coach Cantu dropped it off at my house. Highly unusual. I told him he just should have scanned it and e-mailed it to me."

This is a man who rarely carries a phone. There's no way he has a scanner.

"I'm graduating?" I ask, and Leo tries to sit up a little too quickly and we're wobbling again. He finally stretches across the entire hammock sideways with his hands on the ground on one side and his feet on the ground on the other side. He's turning and looking at me with wide eyes.

"Well, yes. And you're still the salutatorian."

I squeal so loud that Mr. Spencer lets out a string of curses I know he wishes he could take back.

"Practice is Monday morning. You'll need to be there a little early so we can run through the opening."

"Yes, sir!" I say, ending the call after we say our good-byes.

I throw myself at Leo and as he flips over to catch me, we pitch completely off the hammock and land in the thick green grass.

"Did I hear what I think I did?" he says.

I'm nodding and laughing and crying. He holds me close and I bury my face in his neck. His hands run through my hair and he's telling me how proud of me he is and it's more than I can take.

Pulling away from each other slightly, we're face-to-face for about five seconds and then we're kissing. His hands wrap around me, tugging me in closer, and mine latch on to him like I'll never let him go.

When I remember we are in full view of the back windows of my house, I break the kiss and bury my face once again in the crook of his neck.

"You know what this means," Leo says.

A million things run through my head as I wonder where he's going with this.

"We both lost out on first-place finishes."

And we're laughing. And it feels so good.

"Why do you think he signed it?" I ask.

He shrugs. "Want to go ask him?"

I'm up before he's finished his question. "Yes, I do. After all that, I want to know. Will you ride with me?"

He gets up, pulling my hand into his. "Of course."

I drive us to the club without bothering to call. There's no way to know if Coach Cantu's even going to be there, but I can't wait.

The guy at the guard station waves me through before I

come to a complete stop, and it doesn't take long to find Coach Cantu. He's sitting at one of the round metal tables on the patio of the clubhouse, a notebook and calendar spread out in front of him.

"Coach Cantu?" I say, and he looks up at me when he hears his name.

He gives me a smile and says, "Olivia, how are you?" And then he notices Leo behind me. His face lights up. "And congratulations on your finish yesterday, Leo. I wasn't sure you were going to pull it off with your rough start."

Okay, that's like salt in the wound.

"Just had to get my head back on right," Leo says.

Coach's eyes bounce between Leo and me a few times. "What can I do for you this morning?"

"I wanted to thank you. For signing my form," I say. I'm nervous but I don't know why. "After the text you sent, I thought for sure you wouldn't, since I didn't finish my hours." Maybe I'm half expecting him to chew me out for almost wrecking the tournament for Leo.

He gives me a tight smile. "I wasn't sure what this week would be like when you showed up here. When I sent you that text, the officials had not informed me as to what happened and I thought you were a no-show. And I'll admit, I was furious. But when I found out what happened, I realized you had finally understood the most essential part of golf. Integrity. All players are required to keep their own score and call penalties on themselves. It's the most important principle. Without it, the rest doesn't matter. When I heard what you did, what you admitted to, even though you didn't have to and at some peril to yourself, I thought, *She finally gets it!*"

I can't look at him. I know I'm blushing, I can feel it.

"So I signed the form and turned it in for you. Mr. Spencer said he'd let you know, but I should have called you myself."

I swallow the lump in my throat. "I'm so sorry I blew your class off. If there's one thing I regret, it's that."

He smiles. "Thank you. And good luck with everything." Then he leans forward to look at Leo. "I'll be watching out for you! You're going to do great things!"

And now Leo is blushing. We're pretty adorable, I must say.

We say our good-byes and walk hand in hand back to the parking lot.

"I guess you need to let your family know," he says once we're back in my car. "That'll take the rest of the day."

I laugh. "Watch this."

Pulling my phone out, I open up a new text to Nonna.

ME: Great news! Coach Cantu signed my form! I get to graduate!

I show Leo the screen and hit SEND. He seems a little confused.

"Just wait."

It only takes about sixty seconds for the texts to start rolling in.

MOM: You got it signed??? Call me!!

AUNT EILEEN: So glad I didn't have to hunt that coach down and give him a piece of my mind! Love you!

UNCLE MARCUS: Happy for you

And on and on it goes. God, I love my family.

FAIRFIELD HIGH SCHOOL

*Commencement
Ceremony*

WEDNESDAY,
MAY 18TH

2:00 p.m.

Wednesday, May 18th

Graduation Day

Our graduation is taking place in the convention center down-town. They put a stage in just for this occasion and we're all seated, facing the crowd of family and friends. Not that we can really see them with the lights pointed at us, blinding us to everything behind them.

I know my entire family is in the audience since Uncle Michael and Tim got here three hours early to stake out enough seats for everyone. And Leo is here and that makes me so incredibly happy. We've planned to visit each other through-out the summer, and it's only a couple of months before we're both in Baton Rouge.

Mr. Spencer walks up to the podium and the crowd gets quiet.

"It's my pleasure to introduce our salutatorian, Olivia Perkins, who will welcome everyone here."

There is loud applause, which makes me blush as I walk to the microphone. I place my notes on the podium and take a deep breath.

"As salutatorian, it's my job to welcome everyone to the commencement exercises! To all our parents and family and friends, I thank you for being here. Thank you for supporting us and cheering us on. We couldn't have gotten here without you.

"I was lucky enough to get the honor of welcoming you here by graduating second in the class. I had to maintain a high enough GPA to beat out every other person on this stage . . . but one," I say, nodding to where Daniel Vegas, the valedictorian, is sitting, and I get a nice chuckle from the crowd. "But I almost didn't make it up here. There was this not-so-bright idea I had to take off-campus PE even though those closest to me knew it would be a disaster. And it almost was. You see, I thought the hard classes—the AP classes— were the only ones that deserved my attention. Those were the only ones that mattered. But I was so wrong. While good grades were the sole requirement for me to make it up here on this stage, holding this honor, I don't think that's how it should be. There is so much more to high school than that. So many more things that are just as important. So now I'd like to ask a few people to join me up here."

I get *a look* from Mr. Spencer as I take my speech off the rails. "Marcus Washington, would you please join me?" Glancing back at the students sitting behind me, I can see they're bewildered. But thankfully, Marcus gets up from his seat and weaves his way through. Once he's next to me, I give him a smile and say to the crowd, "Marcus was the leading receiver for our football team. He broke three state records and will be playing D1 football in the fall. He was one of the team captains and his enthusiasm and drive helped take the team to a 10–1 season. He deserves to be up here as much as I do."

The applause for Marcus is deafening and several loud whistles pierce the air.

"Will Jemma Calliope please come up here?"

Jemma squeals when I call her name and joins us quickly.

"Jemma is captain of the debate team and led them to state. She's also in Law Studies and argued in mock trial, beating every other team in town. This is not a girl you want to get in an argument with. And she deserves to be up here as much as I do."

Jemma pulls me into a hug. I have to wait for the applause to die down before I can call the next person.

"Will Joey Paderewski please come join us?"

Joey stands up, pumps his fists in the air, and yells, "On my way!"

We all cheer as he jogs up to the podium.

"Joey is one of the most talented artists I've seen. He's already had works shown in galleries and his pieces are hanging in several homes throughout the city. But he also made sure we had the best banners and signs at games and events. He will be attending Savannah School of Art and Design in the fall and I know it's only a matter of time before he's a household name. He deserves to be up here as much as I do."

Joey blows me a kiss and takes a bow for the cheering crowd.

Mr. Spencer is about to lose it, but I have one more I want to do before he forcibly removes me from the stage.

"Will Vanessa Singleton please come up here?"

We all watch Vanessa get up from her seat, a little nervous, but she finally joins us at the podium.

"Vanessa is the editor of our school newspaper and the yearbook. She's worked tirelessly for four years to make sure everything that happens at our school is recorded for history and shared with the school. No one would know of all the great things this class has done if it weren't for Vanessa. She deserves to be up here as much as I do."

Our parents and friends and family are now standing and clapping for all of us. I have to almost scream to be heard over them.

"I could stand up here all day and ask student after student to join us, but I've already blown through my time and there's a really good chance I'll be escorted off soon, so I'll finish by saying I'm honored to share this stage with all three hundred and seventy-seven members of this graduating class. It took all of us to make it. Now let's do this!"

Our small group waves to the crowd as they clap and shuffle back into their seats.

I return to my spot among my classmates and search the audience, knowing it's useless to try to find my family in the sea of faces. Then I turn around and find the ones who are sharing the stage with me. Wes is down the row on one side of me and Charlie is down the row on the other side. They are grinning at me and I wish I could hug them. I know Sophie is out in the audience, but I wish she were up here with us.

Once the ceremony is over, the convention center is pandemonium, with family members trying to locate their graduates for the requisite pictures. Nonna already sent out a text to the whole family, including Wes and Leo, saying we are to meet outside near the giant oak tree. One by one, we all make our way there and the handful of us who just graduated are kissed and hugged and passed through the crowd. Wes's poor parents are sucked up in the middle of this chaos, but they're probably used to it after all these years.

"Okay, everyone!" Nonna yells. "All the graduates get together for a picture!" Those of us in blue robes all move to the center of the group. "Sophie and Leo, that means you, too!"

The Fab Four move to one side with the Evil Joes and their boyfriends on the other, Leo in the middle bridging us all together. We throw our arms around one another and pull in tight. Every aunt and uncle has their phone out to record the moment.

And no matter what the next four or forty years bring, I know everything will be okay as long as I have these people around me.

Acknowledgments

I finished this book in the first few months of the Covid-19 lockdown and it was hard writing about high school graduation and all of those wonderful end-of-high-school traditions and parties while my own son was a senior and missing out on those very experiences. It was especially bittersweet when that same son, Ross, helped me figure out the ending. This book is for all of those seniors. I'm sad your last year of high school didn't end the way you planned, but I know your future is bright!

As always, thank you to my agent, Sarah Davies, for your continued support. I'm grateful you're on my side.

A huge shout-out to my editor, Heather Crowley, and the

entire team at Hyperion. From the editing to the production to the marketing and publicity, I'm so thankful for each and every one of you. Thank you, Lucia Picerno for the beautiful cover art! I love it!

To Elle Cosimano and Megan Miranda, my critique partners who turned into friends who turned into family. Love you both.

I was as clueless about golf as Olivia was, so I definitely needed some help! Thank you to Katherine Webb, Ricky Rogers, and Marshall Laborde for helping me figure out all of the ways Olivia could mess it up. Any and all mistakes made and liberties taken are all on me.

To my friends and family: I'm so grateful for each and every one of you. Thank you for the continued love and support. And a special thank-you to Missy Huckabay, who said, "What if she screws up her off-campus PE?" when I was trying to figure out exactly what this book was going to be about.

A special shout-out to the winner of the Loyola College Prep Preview Party's "Name a character" winner: Gabe Cantu! Thanks for letting me use your name!

The last and biggest thank-you goes to my husband, Dean, and our boys, Miller, Ross, and Archer. I'm so thankful you are mine.